"The best solution is that you and I get married as soon as possible."

At the mention of marriage Josie's mouth fell open. He looked so cool, as though he were discussing the weather—instead of asking an almost complete stranger to marry him.

"Marry you! You must be mad!" Josie exclaimed. She could not believe what she was hearing. But Conan's dark eyes trapped and held her own, and she knew he was deadly serious.

"Mad, no. Practical, yes," he drawled hardily.

"No. Definitely not. Charles was—" Josie had been going to say he was the father of her unborn child, but Conan continued.

"You are to have a child. A Zarcourt. My father wants the child, and he usually gets what he wants. There is no way my father will allow his grandchild to be born out of wedlock...."

JACQUELINE BAIRD began writing as a hobby when her family objected to the smell of her oil painting, and immediately became hooked on the romantic genre. She loves traveling, and worked her way around the world from Europe to the Americas and Australia, returning to marry her teenage sweetheart. Jacqueline now lives in the North of England, with her husband, Jim, and they have two grown sons.

Books by Jacqueline Baird

HARLEQUIN PRESENTS®
1942—THE RELUCTANT FIANCÉE
2029—GIORDANNI'S PROPOSAL

JACQUELINE BAIRD

A Husband of Convenience

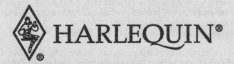

HARLEQUIN®

TORONTO • NEW YORK • LONDON
AMSTERDAM • PARIS • SYDNEY • HAMBURG
STOCKHOLM • ATHENS • TOKYO • MILAN • MADRID
PRAGUE • WARSAW • BUDAPEST • AUCKLAND

ISBN 0-373-12052-4

A HUSBAND OF CONVENIENCE

First North American Publication 1999.

Copyright © 1999 by Jacqueline Baird.

This edition published by arrangement with Harlequin Books S.A.

® and TM are trademarks of the publisher. Trademarks indicated with
® are registered in the United States Patent and Trademark Office, the
Canadian Trade Marks Office and in other countries.

Visit us at www.romance.net

Printed in U.S.A.

CHAPTER ONE

'I'M SORRY, Josie. But Charles is dead.'

'But he can't be. I'm pregnant!' Josie exclaimed, tearing her gaze away from sinfully deep, assessing eyes to glance frantically around the room, unaware of the stunned silence her comment had caused. Her father was seated on the sofa, while Major Zarcourt was at his desk, but there was no sign of Charles Zarcourt. The look of shock on her father's face registered and to her horror she realised she'd spoken out loud, before the sound of sardonic laughter broke the silence.

Her violet eyes swung back to the tall, dark man standing by the drinks cabinet. It was Conan Zarcourt who had delivered the thunderbolt. And, of course, it was Conan who'd laughed! She might have guessed; he must have a penchant for outrageous statements, she thought angrily.

Immaculate in a dark business suit and crisp blue shirt, Conan was leaning against the cabinet with a glass of amber liquid in his hand. As she watched he raised the glass to his mouth and drained it. Then he slammed the empty glass back down with unnecessary force, the expression on his ruggedly attractive face hard to define. He looked more than angry, Josie thought, he looked positively venomous, and for a second she saw a flash of what looked like anguish in his dark eyes. But she must have been mistaken, as he smiled a grim smile.

'Let me get you a drink. You're going to need one,' he offered bluntly.

'No. No alcohol for me. An orange juice.' Even in her

shocked state Josie still had the sense to realise she couldn't drink in her condition.

'As you wish.' Conan's mouth turned down in a wry grimace as he filled a glass with juice and then walked towards her.

He held the glass out to Josie. She looked down at his large hand and back up into his face. Was it only a couple of minutes ago that she'd walked into the study, and been stopped in her tracks by Conan's outrageous response to her casual enquiry, "Has Charles arrived early?"

Her fingers brushed against Conan's as she took the glass he offered, and her hand trembled slightly. What was it about Conan that even when he was at his most vile, cracking stupid jokes about his half-brother Charles, her body reacted alarmingly when he was around?

She stared up at the man towering over her. With thick black hair, broad forehead, a straight, rather large nose, and wide mouth and square jaw, Conan wasn't conventionally handsome; his was a face too rough-hewn for that, but it was still strangely compelling. To her certain knowledge he had visited Beeches Manor only twice in the ten years Josie had lived in the area.

The first time she'd met him she had been looking after the jumble stall at the church summer fair. Charles was supposed to be helping her, but had gone to get her a cold drink when a man impeccably dressed in a three-piece suit had appeared.

'The only thing here that would fit me...is you.' His deep, sexy drawl had shivered along Josie's nerves, giving her goosebumps, and her startled gaze had locked with his for a second, before his eyes had swept over her body in blatant male scrutiny. 'Tell me, are you for sale?' Josie had fought back a chuckle at his cheek, but before she could respond Charles had returned.

'No chatting up the local girls,' Charles had told the

stranger, and much to Josie's surprise he'd slipped an arm around her waist, adding, 'And certainly not mine.'

'I might have guessed,' the man had murmured, and he'd walked away.

'You know him?' Josie had asked Charles.

'You could say that. But never mind him; how about having dinner with me tonight?'

Josie had had a crush on Charles Zarcourt for years, and the disturbing stranger had been forgotten as she'd jumped at the chance of a date with Charles.

Forgotten until the second time she'd seen Conan, when she had almost died of embarrassment.

She dismissed the disturbing memory with a shake of her small head. She could not think about that now. She needed to discover why Conan was here. But then why not? Technically it was his home, she supposed. Conan was right about her needing a drink. Today had been the worst day of her life so far, and she had a horrible feeling in the pit of her stomach that it wasn't going to improve.

She'd taken the afternoon off work and driven from Cheltenham to Oxford to visit the clinic attached to the hospital there, and had her worst fear confirmed. She was pregnant. She had returned home to Low Beeches farmhouse to find an urgent message asking her to go to the Manor House. She had naturally presumed her unofficial fiancé, Charles, had returned from active service in the Army a day early. But looking at the grim faces around her she'd begun to wonder.

Josie took a great gulp of the juice and almost choked as it went down the wrong way, so her father's words barely registered.

'You have to be brave, Josie.'

'Brave,' she murmured. She glanced around again but there was no sign of Charles. Josie blinked and rubbed one damp palm against her thigh. She hadn't eaten all day and was feeling light-headed. Her puzzled gaze sought Conan's. He looked angry and deadly serious, but he couldn't be...

'If this is another one of your outrageous comments masquerading as a joke, Conan, I don't find it funny!' she said curtly.

'No joke. It's true. There's been an accident. Charles *is* dead,' he affirmed, his glittering dark eyes holding her own.

She stared at him in disbelief, all the colour draining from her face. 'An accident?' Josie repeated parrot fashion. There certainly had been an accident, and she was carrying it. Nervously she licked her dry lips. Charles dead! It was unthinkable and, raising the glass to her mouth, she downed the rest of her juice.

She hardly noticed Major Zarcourt's, 'Thank God for small mercies,' before darkness enveloped her, and for the first time in her life she fainted.

Her eyes fluttered open minutes later; she wasn't sure where she was, or what had happened, only aware of the strong arm around her shoulders and the comforting feel of the broad chest her head rested upon.

Then her memory flooded back. Someone had said Charles was dead. But he couldn't be; she was pregnant with his child. She stiffened guiltily. Horrified at her purely selfish thought and raising her head, she jerked out of Conan's protective hold to sit tensely on the edge of the sofa, her hands clasped tightly together in her lap. She glanced at her father sitting beside her, his elbows resting on his knees, head in hands. She turned back to Conan. She did not need to ask the question. The answer was there in the compassion that was evident in his dark eyes.

'Is it true?' she demanded unevenly.

Conan covered her hands with his own large hand and squeezed lightly as he replied. 'I'm sorry, Josie, so sorry, but yes.'

She wanted to cry—she should cry—but the tears would not come, not yet...

'How did it happen?' she managed to ask almost normally, and, shrugging his hand away, she sat up straighter, amazed at her own control.

'Don't think about it now, Josie. Are you all right? That's the important thing,' he prompted.

'Yes. Yes, I'm fine, but please, I want to know,' she demanded, her glance sliding from one man to the other in her agitation. Major Zarcourt was sitting in the hard-backed chair behind his desk, while Conan, her father, and herself were seated in a row on the sofa—like the Three Stooges, she thought wildly, before her eyes were drawn back to Conan's face, waiting for his answer.

'I think I should let my father explain. I'm sure he can tell you the correct story much better than I,' Conan drawled cynically, lounging back against the arm-rest, his long body angled towards her, dark eyes ranging slowly over her small face and down over her slender body perched on the edge of the seat.

Josie felt the colour rise in her cheeks, and for a second she remembered the last time she'd seen Conan. But now was not the time to give way to embarrassment, and deliberately she turned her attention to the Major. Then she listened in mounting horror as he confirmed Charles's death.

Two days ago, while travelling in a Jeep, Charles had driven over an unmarked landmine. He'd died instantly. The family had been informed at lunchtime, but as Josie had not been at work all afternoon they hadn't been able to contact her.

A lump lodged in her throat, threatening to choke her. Her lovely eyes glistened with unshed tears as the Major's voice droned on.

'It was the way he would have wanted to go. On active service with his regiment. He was a hero.'

She heard the words, but all Josie could think of was poor Charles. All her doubts about him were put aside as the desperate horror of his death hit her. Charles—blond, blue-eyed, handsome Charles—was dead. It was unbelievable. So swamped was she by the enormity of what had happened and all its ramifications, she saw nothing odd in the Major's next words and answered him without thinking.

'Tell me, Josie, is it true? Are you carrying Charles's child? Is it confirmed?'

'Yes, I was at the clinic this afternoon; that's why you couldn't find me,' she explained, her tears overflowing and slowly running down her soft cheeks.

'My God! Father, can't you see the girl is in shock?' Conan prompted scathingly. 'Are you really so desperate that you have to question the poor girl at a time like this?'

Poor girl indeed! Conan's comment was just what she needed to stop herself wallowing in self-pity. She might have just lost her boyfriend, and be pregnant, but no one was going to call her a 'poor girl', and certainly not an arrogant devil like Conan.

'I'm taking her home.' Conan's voice penetrated her chaotic thoughts. Raising her head, she saw the derisory glance he flicked at her father before he added, 'She is your daughter, Mr Jamieson. Instead of sitting there as if the weight of the world rested on your shoulders, you could try looking after her. She sure as hell needs someone to.'

'No. No.' Josie finally found her voice and, jumping to her feet, she brushed the tears from her eyes with the back of her hand.

She was a small girl, just five feet tall, but perfectly proportioned. Her blue-black hair hung in a profusion of curls down past her shoulders. Her violet eyes were large and outlined with thick sooty lashes, her nose was small and straight, her mouth full-lipped and gently curving. Dressed in a simple blue cashmere sweater, a colour-coordinated short straight skirt that ended some four inches above her knees, and her feet encased in classic navy blue high-heeled pumps, she had no idea how lovely she looked, or how courageous, to the three men whose startled eyes were fixed upon her.

'You're in shock, Josie.' Conan unfolded his impressive length from the sofa, and in one lithe stride was beside her. 'Let me take you home; your father is in no state to drive.'

Her father might not be, but no way was she letting Conan take her home. She remembered the last time he had driven her to the farmhouse all too clearly. He had made it very obvious he didn't approve of her relationship with Charles, and she didn't need his false sympathy.

'No thank you. I am perfectly capable of driving.' Turning to look at her father, she added, 'Come on, Daddy. I'll drive us home.'

A large hand curved around her upper arm. 'Don't be stupid, Josie; you're in shock. Let me...'

'Let go of me!' she cried, and violently she pulled her arm free from Conan's grasp, staggering slightly as she did so. 'I don't need your help.' Again turning to where her father still sat, she added, 'Please, Dad. I want to leave.' The trauma of the last few weeks, the doctor's confirmation of her pregnancy this afternoon, and the ultimate irony— the death of Charles—were threatening to make her break down completely. She had to get away from Beeches Manor, and more importantly she had to get away from Conan.

Luckily her father, finally sensing her real need to leave, agreed.

How she drove the old Ford car home she would never know. Tears blurred her eyes, but whether they were for herself or Charles she wasn't completely sure.

Later that night, Josie lay in her small bed, unable to sleep. The events of the past few weeks flickered through the windmills of her mind in a series of brief pictures, ending with the tragic death of Charles Zarcourt. Their engagement was supposed to have been made official this weekend. But Josie knew, if she was honest with herself, that she'd had every intention of cancelling the arrangement. Within days of Charles's departure, she had realised she didn't love him. Like thousands of girls before her, she'd been blinded by a romantic ideal and had made a stupid mistake. It was only when she'd begun to suspect she might be pregnant that the full enormity of her mistake had been brought home to her. Even so she'd decided there was no way she was marrying Charles. Her plan had been to explain to Charles in person when he arrived tomorrow—Friday—and hope he would understand. But not any more. He was dead... But from deep in her subconscious a devilish little feeling of relief surfaced. She'd been spared the arguments that refusing to marry Charles would have fuelled. And there would have been arguments, simply because her father and the Major had been friends for years.

Charles and his father lived at the Beeches Manor House not far from the village of Beeches, in the heart of the Cotswolds. After the death of Josie's mother, her father had moved from London and rented Low Beeches farmhouse from the Major. The old men played chess every Tuesday, and Josie had known Charles for ten years and had harboured a schoolgirl crush on him for almost as long. He was not at home very much, but he'd been back for a month in the summer before being posted overseas. He'd asked Josie out three times in all, and she supposed one could say they'd been courting, but only just. Until the fatal night of his going-away party at the Manor House...

Josie stirred restlessly on the bed and groaned out loud as the memory came back to haunt her. It had been the most humiliating experience of her life.

She'd been sad at the thought of Charles leaving, but

hardly broken-hearted. But all that had changed when he'd danced with her, plied her with drinks, and sworn he loved her, wanted to marry her, later leading her to his bedroom and finally into his bed.

Afterwards he'd patted her bottom, leapt off the bed, saying, 'I need a drink,' and had left the room, muttering, 'Stay here; I'll be back in a minute.'

It had been the first time for Josie, and if she hadn't drunk so much it would never have happened. Making love was nothing like she had expected; in fact she had been horribly disappointed. But worse had been to follow.

Suddenly the bedroom door had opened, the light from the hall illuminating a path across the room. She'd hastily sat up and wrapped the sheet firmly around her, wishing she had dressed and left. She'd glanced towards the door and gasped, her mouth falling open in astonishment.

'Very nice—a joke of Charles's no doubt, but I'm not in the mood tonight. Go peddle your wares downstairs, sweetie,' a cynically mocking voice drawled lazily.

It wasn't Charles but a total stranger, although the voice had sounded vaguely familiar. But Josie was not about to hang around to find out who it was. She swung her feet to the floor, desperate to hide anywhere away from the dark man standing in the doorway. Then the bedroom light clicked on.

'You!' he'd exclaimed. 'What the hell are you doing here?' he demanded furiously. His dark eyes took in the rumpled bedclothes and Josie's obvious naked state beneath the sheet she had wrapped clumsily around her.

She looked at him and groaned. It was the man from the church fête. That was all she needed—a sophisticated stranger witnessing her downfall. She did not stop to answer him but, frantically scrambling around on the floor for her clothes, picked them up and made to dash for the bathroom.

Her wrist was caught and held, and he pulled her to a stop. 'Not so fast. I think you owe me an explanation. After all, it isn't every night a man walks into his room and finds a young girl obviously, well…' His dark eyes narrowed, his firm mouth twisting in a knowing sneer. 'I'm sure I don't have to spell it out for you.' His contemptuous gaze skimmed her from head to foot, lingering on the soft curves of her breasts and then back to her bright red face.

'*Your* room?' she cried 'Don't be ridiculous; this is Charles Zarcourt's bedroom! Who on earth do you think you are?' she demanded, her fear giving way to anger. She felt as if she was in a nightmare, and any minute she would wake up. And this very large, very hunky guy was doing nothing for her peace of mind.

'Charles didn't tell you. That doesn't surprise me.' And, bowing his head slightly, he added, 'Allow me to introduce myself. Conan Zarcourt, half-brother to Charles, at your service.' By the cynical gleam in his eye she knew he was relishing her discomfort. 'And you are?' One dark brow arched enquiringly, and he waited…

'Josie—Josie Jamieson.' Why was she even talking to him? she asked herself a second later. Talk about being caught flagrante delicto, she thought with a grim smile. She had never been so humiliated or felt so small in her life. But she was not about to show it.

'Well, Josie Jamieson, I am waiting for your explanation—or perhaps I should ask Charles…?'

'Charles and I are engaged to be married *actually*; not that it is any concern of yours,' she said, forcing herself to meet his eyes. 'It is perfectly normal for engaged couples…' She trailed off, stunned by the thunderous expression on his darkly handsome face.

'But why here? Why now? Why in my bed? I want some answers and you are going to give me them,' he demanded arrogantly.

Was it really his room? She was confused; Charles had said it was his—but she was not going to tell this man that. So instead she said, 'So what if we did use your room! You weren't using it.'

'But I am now, little lady, and I know my half-brother never misses a trick where I am concerned,' he said dryly. 'But what about this engagement? You can't seriously be intending to marry Charles. How old are you? Eighteen, nineteen?'

'Twenty,' Josie said indignantly. Her height and youthful looks were the bane of her life.

'My God! Have you any idea how old he is? Almost forty. He could be your father,' he said scathingly.

'Charles loves me and we are going to be married. Age doesn't matter when you're in love.' Josie mouthed the clichéd words, not really believing them herself. But, dragging her wrist free from Conan's grip, she made a dash for the bathroom. Something caught the sheet that was covering her, and she froze for a second stark naked, her eyes fixed on the elegantly dressed man in the three-piece suit. The contrast couldn't have been more startling. Gulping hard, she ran...

'Very nice.' Conan's deep voice followed her as she continued her headlong flight across the room, and slammed the bathroom door behind her.

Calling herself every kind of fool, she pulled her clothes back on, tidied herself up, all the time wondering why Charles had not introduced her to his half-brother at the church fête. It had never entered her head that they might be related—one so fair and the other so dark. She had thought the dark man looked good but had dismissed him from her mind as a stranger passing through the village.

'Conan Zarcourt.' She said the name softly. It suited him. She hoped it also suited him to have done a vanishing act. She could not hide in the bathroom much longer.

Eventually she walked back into the bedroom, praying Conan would have left. But no such luck.

He had changed from the suit he had arrived in, into a white tee shirt that revealed his strong, tanned arms, dusted with soft black hair, and well-worn blue jeans that hung low on his hips. The zip was fastened but the top snap was undone and gaping.

Josie swallowed hard, and bit down the disloyal thought that he looked a whole lot better than Charles.

'Are you okay?' he demanded, roughly pushing the shirt into his jeans and snapping the fastener. 'I've seen the bed. Your first time… If that bas—'

'Well, well, this is cosy,' a voice smoothly interrupted. 'I see you have met my half-brother Conan, Josie, sorry I took so long.' He held a bottle in his hand.

Josie turned at the sound of Charles's voice and quickly crossed the room to join him at the door. Charles slipped an arm around her waist and pressed a wet kiss on her lips that made her want to wipe her mouth.

'Well, Charles, I gather congratulations are in order. Josie has just told me of your engagement. When is the wedding to be?' Conan asked silkily.

'What did you tell him that for?' Charles demanded angrily of Josie.

'Don't blame the child,' Conan drawled. 'I forced it out of her. You know me, Charles, I always find out in the end, and I'm sure you really wanted me to know.' Fixing Charles with a glacial glance, he added, 'There's no need for embarrassment. We're all family, as you are so keen to remind me every quarter, and Father will be delighted. His eldest son finally getting married.'

Josie was struck dumb as Charles agreed… She didn't understand why he hadn't simply denied they were engaged. She hadn't actually believed Charles's offer of marriage was genuine; she had simply been carried away by the romance of it all—he a soldier off to war, and, more realistically, the drink.

But before anyone could object Conan was leading them downstairs and into the study where he seemed to take a devilish delight in prompting Charles into telling his father that he and Josie were unofficially engaged.

The Major was delighted. Charles appeared equally pleased, and Josie was simply confused. So much so that when Conan insisted on driving her home because Charles was over the limit she made no objection. Her last glimpse of Charles was his blond head bent over a tall, red-headed woman, their arms wrapped around each other. Josie had been introduced to her earlier. She was the wife of Charles's commanding officer.

Josie sat stiffly in the passenger seat of the car, suddenly stone-cold sober. How on earth had she got herself in such a mess? She shot a fulminating glance at the arrogant male at her side. It was all his fault; if he hadn't caught her in his bed and goaded her into saying she was engaged to Charles, she could have put the events of tonight down to experience and tried to forget. But she'd no doubt the Major would tell her father, and she was going to have great trouble explaining her behaviour.

'Your home, I believe,' Conan said coolly as he halted the car outside the door of Low Beeches farmhouse.

Josie hastily unfastened her seat belt and reached for the door handle. 'Thank you,' she mumbled.

'Wait!' The command was curt, and, leaning forward, Conan caught her hand in his much larger one and turned her back to face him.

'What for? I think you've done enough for one night.' She was exhausted, sore and fed up, and when his hand moved to her bare arm she flinched, her skin burning where he'd touched.

'Not so fast. After all, we are soon to be related; surely I merit a brotherly kiss?'

Before she knew what he intended Conan had slipped an arm around her waist and hauled her across his lap. His other hand tangled in her silky black curls, holding her face up to his. She was trapped, her high round breasts crushed against the massive bulk of his chest, and her violet eyes widened in astonishment as his dark head bent and his lips covered hers.

He tasted slightly of mint, his mouth firm but undemanding. Then suddenly he was kissing her with a deeply sensual passion that lit an answering response in her young body. Josie was too astounded by his audacity to do anything other than submit to the expert demand of his mouth. Her body grew soft and pliant against him, his arm tightened around her for an instant, then suddenly she was back in her seat, but too dazed to do anything but stare up at him.

'That was just a sample to compare with, Josie,' And, slipping out of the car, he walked around to the passenger side and helped her out. 'Don't be in too much of a hurry to marry. You don't have to marry the first man you have sex with.'

'How...?'

'Never mind, but remember there are plenty more fish in the sea. Take it from me, you have no chance of a happy-ever-after with Charles.' And he left her standing on the doorstep.

Josie watched him drive off, wishing she had slapped his face or something.

Remembering that night now, Josie sighed heavily. Conan was wrong, she thought wearily as the grey light of dawn glinted through her bedroom window; there were not plenty more fish in the sea, not for her. She was pregnant and destined to be an unmarried mother, and for the first time since discovering the fact she realised she did not mind. The thought of a child of her own to love was somehow comforting, and finally she drifted off to sleep.

Josie yawned and opened her eyes. 'Daddy,' she murmured, the word little more than a croak. Her throat felt dry and rough. He was sitting in the chair by her bed.

'You're awake, Josephine. How do you feel?' he asked quietly, his tired eyes fixed sadly on her small pale face.

'I'm fine,' she smiled. Her father was the only person to call her Josephine. Then, like a shutter falling, the smile was wiped from her face, as the memory of yesterday returned to haunt her. 'What time is it?' she asked, the mundane question masking her very real distress.

'About ten-thirty.'

'Oh, my word! I'm late for work!' she exclaimed.

'No. I have already called your office, and told them you were suffering from a severe migraine.'

'But I never get migraine.'

'Oh, Josephine! What does it matter?' Her father sighed and rose from the chair to sit on the side of the bed. He took her hand in his. 'I am so sorry. I know how hard it must be for you, losing Charles so tragically. I remember how I felt when your mother died. This is all my fault. I feel so guilty. I've let you down—and your mother, God rest her soul! If I'd been a better father, given you the guidance and support you needed, this would never have happened.'

Her father's halting speech made Josie feel worse. She studied his shadowed face in the morning light. Poor Daddy—she had failed him so badly. He'd been so pleased when he'd thought she was going to marry Charles, and she'd not had the nerve to tell him of her own doubt, and now she didn't need to. But she could see the strain etched into the multitude of lines on his much loved face, and she couldn't bear the thought of him blaming himself. The tears welled in her eyes. 'Oh, Daddy,' she whispered, and one tear rolled down her cheek.

'Hush, Josephine; don't cry.' he soothed, wiping her cheek with a large white handkerchief. 'We'll work something out.'

'I hope so,' she murmured. The tears were more for her father than herself; she knew deep down she would manage. But her father was an old-fashioned gentleman, who still considered an unmarried mother a disgrace.

'Trust me, Josephine. Everything will be fine. Take your time, wash your face, get dressed, and then come downstairs. Conan Zarcourt is here and would like to talk to you—about the funeral arrangements I suppose.' With a brief, reassuring squeeze of her hand, he left.

Conan! What did he want? He was a decisive, dynamic man, and she could not imagine why he would want to discuss the funeral with her. Just the thought of the man made her hackles rise. But it also gave her the incentive to get out of bed. She washed and quickly dressed in a pair of grey cords and a black skinny-ribbed jumper. It somehow seemed appropriate; Charles had been her unofficial fiancé, even if she had decided not to marry him, her conscience reminded her. She brushed her hair, and with her face free of make-up she slipped her feet into a pair of mules, and went downstairs. Better to face Conan sooner rather than later…

CHAPTER TWO

SHE stopped at the bottom of the stairs. The hall was square and small, with a door leading off either side, one to the dining room, the other to the sitting room, and to the back of the hall was the kitchen. It was a typical double-fronted stone-built farmhouse from the last century, with low oak-beamed ceilings and walls a foot thick. She guessed Conan would be in the sitting room, and, taking a deep breath to steady her nerves, she opened the door and walked in.

'Josie! How are you today?' Conan's dark eyes swept over her, lingering a fraction too long to be innocent on the proud thrust of her breasts revealed by the clinging knit sweater.

His conventional polite greeting didn't fool Josie for a moment; she doubted very much he was here simply to offer condolences. He had never approved of her relationship with Charles, and the Conans of this world did not waste their valuable time on young girls they didn't like, unless the Major had sent him. But then she couldn't see this man doing anyone's bidding.

He was standing in the middle of the room, his broad-shouldered frame clad in a soft black wool roll-neck sweater and hip-hugging black jeans. The colour, while suitable for a man in mourning for his half-brother, only served to reinforce his innate powerful sexuality. A shiver of not fear but something more basic made the fine hair on her skin stand erect.

'Very well, thank you,' she replied stiltedly, fighting against her peculiar reaction to this man. Then, seeing the

21

cynical twist of his hard mouth, she realised how callous she must sound.

'Well, obliviously not well,' she corrected, 'I mean, Charles is dead, and I...well...' She was babbling, but did not seem able to stop. 'The funeral. You want to discuss...'

'Hush. I understand.' He stepped towards her. Josie tried to step back, his height intimidating her, but she was brought up hard against the closed door.

Conan noted her reaction. His hard mouth twisted faintly and then he turned and strolled across to the nearest arm-chair and lowered himself down onto the seat. He glanced back at her and gestured with one large hand to the sofa opposite. 'Please, Josie, come and sit down; you have nothing to fear from me. I simply want to talk.'

Warily she looked at him; her violet eyes met his bland gaze and she was somewhat reassured.

'The funeral apart, I have something else to discuss with you on behalf of the Major and myself, and it will be in your own best interests to listen.'

She straightened her shoulders and walked across to sit down on the sofa. 'I can't imagine us having anything to discuss, but I'm listening,' she said flatly.

'I know this will be hard for you so soon after hearing of the death of Charles, but I have spoken to my father, and we agreed. Under the circumstances the best solution is that you and I get married as soon as possible.'

At the mention of marriage her mouth fell open. Her eyes widened in shock and looked on the man lounging in her father's armchair, his long legs stretched out before him in nonchalant ease. How did he do it? He looked so cool, so sophisticated, as though he were discussing the weather—instead of asking an almost complete stranger to marry him.

'Marry you! You must be mad!' she exclaimed. She could not believe what she was hearing. Was he joking or what? Surely he could not be that cruel. But his dark eyes trapped and held her own, and she knew he was deadly serious.

'Mad, no; practical, yes.' he drawled hardily.

She lowered her head, avoiding the determination in his eyes. Her gaze skated over his long body. He was all male and somehow threatening. What did he mean? Why on earth would he want to marry her?

'Why?' She was surprised to hear herself ask that. She should have said no and immediately corrected her mistake. 'No. Definitely not. Charles was the—' She got no further as Conan cut in.

'I know Charles was the man you loved.' Actually she'd been going to say he was the father of her unborn child, but she did not correct his assumption as he continued. 'But we have to think of the living, not the dead. You are to have a child. A Zarcourt. Surely you must realise that when you blurted out that you were pregnant in front of my father you lost any chance you had of doing anything about your pregnancy?' he prompted cynically.

'Doing anything about it?' she queried.

Conan shook his dark head. 'I mean an abortion; after all, you can't be more than a few weeks pregnant.'

'Six to be exact,' she fumed. 'And if the Major wants me to have an abortion he can go jump.' The thought had crossed her mind when she'd first discovered her condition, but it hadn't taken a split second for her to dismiss the notion entirely. She could never do such a thing.

'Much as I would like to see my father take a hike—' his lips twitched with amusement '—you misunderstood me. Quite the reverse is true. My father wants the child, and he usually gets what he wants, as you're about to find out. His grief at his eldest son's death is only made bearable by the fact you're carrying his child. There is no way he will allow his grandchild to be born a bastard,' he opined, adding cynically, 'Especially not darling Charles's off-spring.'

Josie was stunned by his words, but, knowing the Major, she could see the truth in his comment. But what she couldn't understand was why he would agree with his father. It was obvious, even from her brief acquaintance with Conan, that there was no love lost between him and his father. This summer had been the first time Josie had ever seen him. He obviously had very little to do with his family.

'But surely you don't agree with him?' she asked. 'I mean, it can't matter to you. You don't even live here.'

'No, I don't, but I should,' he responded bluntly with a degree of bitterness Josie could not fail to recognise. So it was all the more surprising when he asked coolly, 'Do you like living in this house, Josie?'

'Yes. Yes, I do.' What was he talking about now? she wondered, looking around the familiar room, her eyes eventually returning to Conan. He sat forward in his chair, his dark head bent, apparently staring at his hands clasped loosely between his splayed thighs. The only sounds were the steady tick of the grandfather clock and the logs crackling and burning in the open fire.

'This farmhouse was the family home of the Major. He lived here with his first wife—Charles was born here.' He raised his head. 'I don't suppose he told you that?' he queried with a grim smile.

'No, no, he didn't,' Josie said, not sure where the conversation was going.

'I'm not surprised. Contrary to the impression, my father, the Major, likes to give,' he drawled sardonically, 'the Major was not always owner of Beeches Manor. He only acquired that position by marrying my mother. Perhaps if I explain the family history it will answer your question as to why I want to marry you.'

Josie wished he would. She couldn't understand what he

was getting at, or his obvious cynicism. But there was no mistaking the hardness in his eyes, and an implacable determination that Josie found vaguely disturbing.

'My full name is Conan Devine Zarcourt. Conan from the Celtic meaning wisdom, and Devine being my mother's maiden name. For centuries, Devines have owned the Beeches Manor estate, but my grandfather and mother were the last of the line. When she married Major Zarcourt, the Major and Charles moved into the Manor with my mother and grandfather and rented this house out as a holiday home. I was born a year after their wedding, and I don't think it was long after that my mother realised she had made a mistake.

'As a young child I was not aware there was anything wrong in my parents' relationship. But then my grandfather was still alive, and any coldness on my father's part was more than made up for by my grandfather. Plus my mother packed me off to boarding-school when I was seven.'

'How awful for you,' Josie offered; the thought of a young boy away from home at such a tender age seemed so cruel.

One dark brow arched sardonically. 'Sorry to disillusion you, but you are wrong.' His hard-eyed gaze caught hers, denying her sympathy. 'My parents and I were never that close. It was my grandfather I missed. For years I had grown up with the sure knowledge that the Manor would be mine. Grandfather Devine never stopped telling me so. He died when I was eleven, but unfortunately he had signed the Manor over to my mother a few years before he died to avoid death duties, on the strict understanding it was to be held in trust for me, as the only Devine. But my mother had other ideas. As soon as Grandfather died she took off with her lover. Apparently, in her desperation to get a speedy divorce from the Major she agreed to break the trust and sign the Manor over to *him*. She lives in New Zealand now, I believe.'

'But how could she do that?' Josie asked, horrified.

'Quite easily, apparently. When I came of age at eighteen the Major took great delight in telling me the whole story. He had married my mother for the Manor. I was a mistake, a complication he didn't need, and he even questioned my paternity. He'd joined his own farmland to the Manor and managed the whole estate for years, and he intended to go on doing so until Charles showed an interest in it. Then he was going to pass the whole lot on to his eldest and favourite son, and there was absolutely nothing I could do about it—'

'I can't believe your mother or the Major would behave like that,' Josie cut in. She didn't particularly care for the old man, but she couldn't believe he would treat his own child so shabbily.

'Ah, Josie, how you do like to think the best of people. It is one of your many charms,' he said with a wry smile, before adding, 'But, believe me, everything I have told you is the truth. And now, with your help, I have the chance to get my heritage back, and I intend to take it...'

She glanced across at him, her violet eyes caught and held by the burning intensity in the depths of his. Inwardly she shivered. There was something totally implacable about him. As for her helping him, Josie still failed to see what it had to do with her, or why Conan wanted to marry her.

'But with Charles dead you will inherit everything anyway,' she said cautiously, letting her gaze drop to a spot past his shoulder. Perhaps she was still too shocked to think clearly, because she felt she'd missed the point somewhere. But she wasn't about to get embroiled any further. She had enough problems of her own. 'I'm sure it's all very interesting, but it has absolutely nothing to do with me,' Josie continued firmly, straightening her shoulders. She'd no intention of marrying him or anyone else, and it was time she asserted herself.

In one lithe movement Conan left his seat and joined her on the sofa. His closeness unnerved her. Her body tensed as his large hand caught her chin, turning her face to his.

His dark eyes narrowed intently on her face. 'But it has everything to do with you. I know this is a terrible time for you, Josie, and I would do anything to avoid causing you any more pain, believe me.' His face darkened into an expression that made Josie wish she hadn't tried to dismiss him so bluntly. 'But I want what's rightfully mine, and you are the means by which I will get it,' he informed her ruthlessly.

A chill shivered its way down the length of her spine as he dropped his hand from her chin. 'And we must get this settled quickly. Unfortunately time is the one commodity we do not have in your condition.'

Josie grimaced at the reminder.

'Let me spell it out for you. The Major and I had a long talk last night, and we've made a deal. I marry you, give your child the Zarcourt name, and in return I get my rightful inheritance back immediately. Otherwise he will leave everything to you on his death, provided you produce a son; if not, he'll leave it to the church, the dogs' home— anyone other than me.'

Josie was lost for words. She could only gaze at Conan in dumb amazement. He couldn't be serious!

'Well, do you agree? Will you marry me?' he asked, his arm sliding along the back of the sofa and clasping her shoulder. 'Or perhaps, like most women, your mercenary little soul wants to take the chance on giving birth to a son and keeping it for yourself,' he added cynically.

'I would never do that!' Josie cried, finally finding her voice, insulted that Conan should even think such a thing. 'I don't have a mercenary bone in my body,' she informed him, jerking around to the side and shrugging his hand off her shoulder in the process.

'In that case, Josie, what's the difference? One Zarcourt is as good as another to be a father to your child, and at least it will keep the poor kid in the family.'

Her breath caught in her throat at the sheer arrogance of his brutally realistic comment. 'That's totally stupid. You can't just walk in here and say you want to marry me, simply to get your hands on the Manor House. Anyway, what the Major is suggesting isn't fair. You are his son, you are entitled to the estate. You shouldn't be forced to marry me to get it.'

'Not much is fair in this world, Josie, as I think you're beginning to find out,' he offered dryly, before adding, 'But there's no force involved on my part. I want to marry you. You're a very lovely girl, and I can think of a hundred more selfish reasons for wanting you as my wife.'

She closed her eyes for a second, his words forcibly reminding her of the hopelessness of her own situation. When she opened them he was watching her, the expression in his dark eyes, so oddly flecked with gold, seeming sincere, and yet there was something more she could not name in their mysterious depths. She was tempted to agree to marry him. It would solve all her problems. But the memory of the one night she'd spent with Charles rose up in her mind, and she did not fancy repeating the experience. She couldn't...

'So what is it to be, Josie? You help me and I swear I will take great care of you.'

'I couldn't. I hardly know you. I—well...' She slid to a halt, unable to find the words. He said he thought she was lovely and he had other reasons for wanting to marry her. Did he expect her to go to bed with him ? She didn't know and she wasn't about to ask. As far as she was concerned

it wasn't an option. But as if he could read her mind Conan
went on.

'If it's sharing a bed with me that's bothering you, forget
it. Not that I wouldn't mind if you did.' He gave her a very
masculine grin. 'But I promise I wouldn't dream of making
you do anything you didn't want to. You have my word
on it.'

Josie wasn't sure she believed him. It struck her quite
forcibly that Conan wasn't the sort of man to be celibate
for very long. In her friend Zoe's parlance the man was hot
and even Josie, who was off sex for life, could sense the
virile sexuality of the man. So it followed he must have a
girlfriend somewhere. No sooner had the thought entered
her head than she was voicing it.

'But surely a man of your age must have a woman in
his life, someone who might object to you up and marrying
an almost total stranger?' Josie was young but she wasn't
stupid. She'd seen the way Conan looked at her, and she
doubted very much he went through life like a monk.

'No, there is no one of any importance, but if you're
asking for my sexual history I've had two what you might
call long-term relationships, neither of which included sharing my home with the lady in question.' His dark eyes fixed
on her flushed face. 'You, on the other hand, will share my
home when we marry, and you can count on my fidelity as
much as I can count on yours. Satisfied?'

'As long as it is only your home and not your bed,' she
said bluntly, not entirely sure she liked his answer.

'Good. I knew you would see sense. Now, if you have
no further questions I will get everything arranged.'

'Wait a minute. I never said I would marry you.' She
eased a little further back along the sofa, putting more space
between them. 'I need time to think.'

He noted her furtive shuffle with the sardonic arch of
one black brow. 'Take as long as you like.' And, glancing

at the fine gold watch on his wrist he added, 'As long as it's no more than sixty seconds.'

Arrogant devil, she thought, but she also thought of her father, and the worry she was causing him, and her unborn child. How easy it would be to pass all her troubles on to someone else's shoulders, and Conan's were broad enough, she thought, glancing at his physique—so strong, so protective. But…and it was a big but…she didn't love Conan, and he didn't love her. But then she had thought she'd loved Charles, and look where that had got her. In this mess. She wasn't a coward, and she wasn't afraid of hard work. She had looked after her ageing father for the past few years as well as holding down a job.

The trouble, Josie realised, was that it was a catch-22 situation. She was damned if she did and damned if she didn't. If she refused to marry Conan and her child was a boy, the estate would come to her, and she would look like the worst kind of gold-digger. If she did marry Conan just for the sake of the baby, was that any better?

She wanted the very best for her child, and if that meant living with Conan for a year or so, would that be so bad? She thought of her father earlier, blaming himself for her predicament, feeling guilty because he was convinced he had neglected her in some way and betrayed his late wife's trust. It would put her father's mind at ease if she married Conan, she knew. The Major and Conan would be satisfied, and realistically her one brush with sex had put her off for life. She could not see herself falling in love and marrying in the normal course of events, not any more…

'If, if I agreed…' His dark eyes flared triumphantly, and one of his large hands caught her left hand in his. Josie shivered. 'I said *if*,' she reiterated. 'I need to know a lot more about the nuts and bolts of the arrangement. For example, I have a job.'

Conan squeezed her hand. 'Josie, I know you're a legal secretary at Brownlow's law firm in Cheltenham, and I would never deprive you of a career. You are simply creating difficulties where none exist. Ours will be a straightforward marriage of convenience.'

'A marriage of convenience,' Josie murmured. She liked the sound of that. 'A straightforward business arrangement, you mean?' she asked glancing up at him.

'Of course,' he confirmed lightly, his dark eyes holding hers.

'In that case, yes, all right.' She could live with that for the benefit of her child.

'Good. I'm glad we are agreed. Now, for the sake of the Major and your own father, it would obviously be better if you came and lived in my house in London until after the birth of your child.'

'Wait a minute.' Josie pulled her hand from his. '*Move?* I thought the whole idea was you wanted the Manor and you just agreed I could keep my job?'

Conan sat back on the sofa. 'I do want the Manor, but have you looked at the place lately? My father has not spent a penny on it in years. It needs a complete overhaul, and until that is done London is the obvious place to be as my work is there. As for your job—what I said was, I would never deprive you of a career. In principle, I believe in a woman working, fulfilling her potential. But you'd have to leave your present job in a few months anyway when your condition becomes obvious, and you don't need me to tell you what the gossip mill is like around here.'

He was right about the gossip; the locals would be counting the days from the wedding to the birth. Not that Josie cared. But her father would and Conan might. She had rarely heard his name mentioned—he was obviously the expert at avoiding gossip, and she had a vague idea he'd lived abroad for a long time. Suddenly Josie realised she knew very little about him. 'What do you actually do?' she blurted.

'Come now, Josie, surely you know.' he prompted.

'No, I don't,' she snapped back, aware of the cynicism in his tone.

'I work in a bank,' he replied. 'A merchant bank.'

'Oh, my father did that until he retired.' And somehow the thought that Conan and her father shared the same career made Josie feel more kindly disposed towards him.

'I own the bank.'

Josie's mouth dropped open in shock. 'What?' she exclaimed.

'My grandfather left me some shares which my father could not get his hands on. At twenty-one I inherited a sizable block of shares in a merchant bank. I went to London, worked hard and got the opportunity to buy a controlling interest, and I took it. I expanded the business to the USA with branches in New York, Chicago and Los Angeles, which is why for the past few years I've lived mostly in America.'

Glancing at him, Josie could easily believe him. He looked dangerous, his hard features curiously remote, but his eyes were watchful and incredibly dark. 'You must be rich. I never knew,' she said, astonished by his revelation.

As he caught her stunned expression, Conan's lips curved in a grim smile. 'I don't suppose there was any reason why you should. The Major seems to think working in the city is slightly disreputable,' he drawled mockingly. 'But someone in our beleaguered family had to make money.'

Something clicked in Josie's mind. That fateful night of the party. Charles had gone quiet when Conan had mentioned the end-of-quarter accounts. Surely he did not keep Charles and his father supplied with money? 'You helped support Charles—?' She was cut off before she could finish the question.

'For heaven's sake, Josie, can we get down to basics?' Conan interrupted harshly, and, jumping to his feet, he prowled around the small room before returning to stand in front of her.

His hard, chiselled features were still, almost brooding. His dark eyes locked with hers, and his expression was impossible to read. 'How many people have you told about your engagement to Charles?'

'No one,' she answered, too surprised by his outburst and change of subject to prevaricate.

A dark brow climbed quizzically. 'No one, not even you colleagues at work, your friends?'

'No.' Josie felt the colour rise in her cheeks, and tried to justify her reticence. 'You were there that night you heard Charles tell your father; it was to be unofficial until...' She swallowed remembering what had happened to Charles and what day it was. 'Well, until he was supposed to return—today.' She lowered her eyes from his knowing gaze.

'You do surprise me! A woman who can keep a secret about her personal life. I thought you would have bragged to all and sundry you had caught the county's most eligible bachelor.'

'Sorry to disappoint you but I didn't.' Not for a million pounds was she going to admit it was because she had intended calling the whole thing off. Even discovering she was pregnant had not persuaded her to marry Charles.

'So only your father, the Major and I know about your engagement to Charles. You're absolutely sure?' he demanded.

'Yes,' she repeated, glancing briefly back up at him and wondering why it was so important.

'Great.' A triumphant gleam shone in his golden eyes.

'And it's a safe bet Charles never mentioned it to anyone so that makes everything much easier.' He slid one hand into his pocket.

Why was he so certain Charles had kept it a secret? Josie wondered, but she was distracted as her eyes involuntarily followed his hand and she gulped as the fabric of his jeans pulled taut across his thigh outlining exactly how masculine he was. Appalled at the direction her thoughts had taken, she scrambled to her feet, and stepped past him, her face burning. Then, turning and tilting her head to look up at him, she managed to ask, 'Why easier?'

He withdrew a small box from his pocket. 'Simple, Josie.' Opening the box, he caught her hand and slipped an exquisite diamond and sapphire ring in an antique setting on the third finger of her left hand.

Josie looked at the ring, and up at Conan, and back at the ring. He had certainly come prepared, she thought, angry at his arrogant assumption that she would accept his proposal. 'But…'

'No buts, Josie. It's perfect. You and I are engaged. If anyone asks, we met in August at the church fair. You took yesterday afternoon off to have lunch with me, and we got engaged. Then imagine our horror when we returned to the Manor to hear that Charles had died. It's perfect. We will attend the funeral on Tuesday as a couple, and we have a perfect excuse for a small, quiet wedding—we are in mourning for Charles.'

She had thought he was ruthless but, listening to Conan, she realised he was diabolically devious. It all fitted, and yet she wanted to dent his superior male attitude. 'What about the clinic I visited?'

'So what? How long were you there—an hour, two? And did you tell the doctor the name of the father? Somehow I think not.'

He was right again. She had deliberately travelled to

Oxford, where no one knew her, and had spent most of the afternoon sitting in a coffee bar deciding what to do.

'No, I didn't,' Josie admitted, and closed her eyes, overcome by sadness for poor Charles. When she opened them again, Conan was slowly assessing every one of her features, from her flushed face to her small hand that wore his ring. He gently caught her hand and, raising it to his lips, kissed her fingertips.

'Don't worry, Josie; you won't regret marrying me, and it's the best for everyone. Believe me.'

Josie snatched her hand back; the touch of his lips on her skin disturbed her, more than she wanted to admit. 'Oh, I do… You have everything worked out beautifully,' she snapped sarcastically. 'And hey! We can always get divorced once…' She stopped; she could hardly say when the Major died or when Conan had Beeches Manor—it sounded too callous, even if it was true.

Conan slanted her a sardonic glance. 'You're quite right. But let's get married first, hmm?'

'Yes.' For the sake of her unborn child, and her father's peace of mind, she would do anything. Marrying Conan could not be that bad, she told herself. He said he spent a lot of time in America so she might hardly ever see him.

'Good. I am glad we understand each other. I have to leave now but I'll be back to take you to dinner on Monday night. As I said, the funeral is on Tuesday and we'll go together.'

She never got a chance to answer as her father walked into the room. He looked at Josie, then at Conan.

'When is the funeral? Have you got it all organised?'

'Yes, Mr Jamieson—on Tuesday at two. But I need to speak to you on another matter.' And, suddenly snaking an arm around Josie's waist, he hauled her into his side. Josie tensed and tried to ease away from his iron grip, but his fingers dug sharply into her side, as a warning.

'Your daughter has kindly agreed to be my wife, and I want your blessing,' Conan said smoothly, bending his dark head towards Josie and brushing his lips along her brow, before clasping her hand and lifting it to show her father the ring on her finger.

'Is this true, Josephine? You are engaged to Conan?' Her father turned puzzled eyes on her flushed face. 'Are you sure you know what you're doing?'

Conan's fingers dug deeper in her flesh. 'Yes—yes, Daddy,' she said, forcing a smile to her lips.

'I love your daughter, Mr Jamieson, and I want to take care of her.' Conan's dark eyes lingered lovingly on her small face. 'And she has made me the happiest man in the world today.'

Josie stared in dumb amazement at Conan. Talk about over the top! Her father would never believe that. She glanced at her father, and she was stunned to realise he half did...

'Do you really think you will be happy, married to Conan?' he queried, his pale eyes, hazed with concern, clinging to hers. 'You don't have to rush into marriage, you know.'

'But I want to, Daddy' she said firmly, and, making herself look up into Conan's dark face, she added, 'I have no doubt at all; I adore Conan.'

'Well, if you're sure Josephine,' he said, his glance lingering on her. 'And you do look better—you have some colour back in your face.'

The colour was the result of anger at being pressed from leg to shoulder against the hard heat of Conan's body. But the relief in her father's eyes prevented her from disillusioning him. 'I'm sure, Daddy,' she said through clenched teeth.

'In that case, Conan, of course you have my blessing. It was good of you to ask me.'

Josie looked at her father's smiling face and was amazed at his blindness. Conan had not asked, he had told him. Surely he'd heard the sarcasm in Conan's tone? But apparently not.

'I am so happy for you both,' her father continued. 'The death of Charles is a tragedy, but there is no point in adding tragedy upon tragedy. Josephine is a very lucky girl.'

Lucky was not how she would have put it, Josie thought as she pulled her hand free of Conan's and he finally let her move from his side, only to find herself enfolded in her father's arms as he hugged her tightly.

'It's a miracle, Josephine. I told you everything would be fine.' Her father patted her on the head, walked over to his armchair and sat down. 'Have you seen my paper?' he asked.

Josie hated being patted on the head. It only accentuated her tiny stature in her mind, and added to the simmering resentment she felt against the two men in the room. She marched to the occasional table where the daily paper lay and picked it up. She was tempted to hit her dad over the head with it. Much as she loved her father, he was the world's worst chauvinist; her opinions didn't matter at all in comparison to Conan's. She flashed an exasperated glance at her father's down-bent head, then, turning, caught the gleam of wicked humour in Conan's eyes.

'Let me show you out,' she snapped. She had a nasty suspicion Conan might turn out to be even more of a chauvinist than her father. Walking out into the hall, she opened the front door and stood back, expecting Conan to leave.

'On my way over here this morning I was convinced I would have to bully you into listening to me,' he confided as he stopped in the doorway, his large body almost filling the space. 'I'm intrigued to discover you do possess some common sense after all, and I am delighted you have agreed to be my wife.'

'*After all...*' The nerve of the man! He had obviously thought she was an impulsive fool from the minute he'd met her. Well, she would prove him wrong, and be the perfect social wife, while giving her baby the very best start in life. 'Yes, well, it is just business,' Josie said firmly.

'Of course, but take good care of the ring; it was my grandmother's.' His dark eyes slid down the length of her body with a possessive gleam in their golden depths, making Josie shudder inside, and for a second she questioned if his intentions really were platonic. His long, tanned fingers closed around her wrist, and she thought he was going to check the ring, but he surprised her completely by folding her hands behind her back, and easing her into close contact with his long body.

'What...?' she tried to pull her hands free.

'Don't look so frightened, Josie.' Conan let go of her wrists. 'I'm simply going to seal our deal with a kiss.' Lowering his head, he closed his mouth gently over hers. His hands curved over her shoulders, and then swept lightly over her breasts and around her waist, holding her firm.

To Josie's shame she felt her traitorous body responding. How could she? she thought wildly, and, turning her head away from his searching lips, she placed her hands on his chest and pushed as hard as she could.

'Business, remember, a marriage of convenience, you said!' Her eyes were shooting sparks, but, when they clashed with his, to her fury he was grinning.

'True, but we must present the right image of a loving couple—at least until the child is born. The odd kiss will be unavoidable, and it seems to me you need the practice.' he chuckled. 'See you Monday,' and he left, spinning on his heel.

Stunned, Josie simply stared at his retreating back as he walked down the short path to the road. It was only when he turned to give her a jaunty wave that she realised what she was doing, and slammed the front door. She had a horrible feeling she might have just made the biggest mistake of her life...

CHAPTER THREE

WHEN the telephone rang on Saturday morning, Josie was having second, third and fourth thoughts about the advisability of a marriage of convenience to a man like Conan. Unfortunately, she discovered very quickly it was too late to get out of it. The caller was Zoe, her friend from work.

'You sly dog, Josie! Migraine, my eye...' Zoe's voice echoed down the line. 'What was it? A hot night of passion that spun over into the morning? But I do think you could have told me. I had no idea you were even going out with a man, let alone getting engaged.'

'How did you know?' Josie asked when she could get a word in, not at all sure who Zoe thought she was engaged to...

'Oh, please, Josie. The engagement is announced between Miss Josephine Jamieson, only daughter of...blah, blah, and Mr Conan Devine Zarcourt, blah, blah, blah. It's in this morning's *Times*. Mind you, I didn't know that Conan Zarcourt lived at Beeches Manor. And how come you never even mentioned him to me?'

Josie could not believe it. After listening to Zoe ramble on, and promising to tell her the full story at work on Monday, Josie finally put the phone down, and went looking for her father.

Five minutes later her worst fear was realised. With a bit of judicious questioning of her dad she'd discovered the Major had already prepared the announcement of her engagement to Charles the day he'd learned of his death. Then he had been so upset he had left Conan to see to all the arrangements.

Her father chuckled. 'Obviously Conan has simply substituted his own name for Charles's. You've got a good man there, Josephine—clever and quick-thinking,' he remarked happily, and for the second time in two days she felt like hitting him.

Instead she went for a long walk across the fields to try and calm down. She could not blame her father; he belonged to a different generation. He had been over fifty when Josie was born, her mother forty-two. Her mother had died when she was ten, and right now Josie would have given anything to have her mother to talk to.

What she got was dozens of calls all day Saturday, congratulating her on her engagement. On Sunday, when news of Charles's death appeared in the newspaper, quite a few of the calls congratulated her and then offered condolences too, saying the timing was unfortunate, but could not be helped.

By Monday evening Josie was spitting nails. She had spent a terrible day at work; Zoe had insisted on hearing the whole story, and Josie hated lying. Everyone in the Cheltenham law firm had congratulated her, including Mr Brownlow himself, and she had felt a complete fraud, especially when sympathy for the death of Charles was expressed.

When the doorbell rang at seven-thirty she stormed across the hall and flung open the door, ready to give Conan a blasting.

'You! I'm surprised you dare show your face,' she snarled, and almost slammed the door in his face.

'Is that any way to greet your fiancé?' Conan mocked. His dark eyes swept over her slender form with studied male appreciation, taking in her flushed, angry face and the tumble of black curls falling around her shoulders. His gaze lingered on her simple red sweater dress that clung to her every curve, then moved down to her shapely legs, to her feet encased in three-inch high-heeled black shoes, and then back to her face. 'Very nice and very sexy,' he murmured softly, a slow sensual smile tilting his firm lips.

She had forgotten how dynamic he appeared in the flesh. He exuded a raw animal magnetism which his casually tailored black suede jacket and hip-hugging moleskin trousers seemed designed to enhance. She had always thought him attractive, but tonight, with his black hair tussled by the evening breeze, there was a sense of power about him, a vitality that sent a frisson of fear down her spine.

'Josie, either ask me in or let's go.'

She blinked and, lifting her eyes, she caught the amusement lurking in the depths of his. He knew very well she was mad, and thought it funny.

'Go...? I'd like to tell you where to go! What did you mean—?' she began.

'Josie, Josie, please. Not on the doorstep.' And, brushing past her, he picked up her jacket and purse off the chair where she had placed them, and, with a hand at her back, urged her down the path to where his car was parked. 'Here, put this on. November nights can be cold.'

She allowed him to slip her jacket over her shoulders and took her purse from his outstretched hand. 'I want an explanation.'

'Later.' He opened the passenger door and gestured for her to get in the car. 'I don't believe in arguing and driving at the same time.' Walking around to the driver's side, he slid in behind the wheel, and started the engine.

Josie knew what he said made sense, so, silently fuming, she watched him drive the car along numerous country roads until he pulled up outside a small country pub called The White Swan.

'This is the first pub I had a drink in as a boy,' Conan remarked, turning in his seat to look at her in the dim light of the small car park. 'I think you'll like it; the food is good.'

'If you say so,' Josie said grudgingly, and felt for the car door.

'Wait,' Conan commanded, and caught her hand in his. 'Say what you have to before we go inside.' He was idly stroking her palm with his thumb as he spoke. 'I have no intention of arguing with you while we eat.'

His touch was sending tiny quivers of sensation over her sensitive flesh and it took a supreme effort of will not to tear her hand away. But she could not afford to show him any sign of weakness. Conan would try any trick in the book to get his own way—and some he had personally invented, Josie was sure.

'All right. Explain to me how the announcement of our engagement got in the newspaper so fast, and don't bother lying, because I know.'

'If you know, why ask?' he mocked.

'You know damn well what I mean.'

'Don't curse, Josie; I don't like that in a lady.'

'Tough, because you're enough to make a saint curse,' she shot back.

'All right, I admit it. My father had prepared the announcement of your engagement to Charles on Thursday. He asked me to deal with it, and I did.'

'He had no right to,' Josie snapped, unaware of what she was revealing.

Conan's hand grasped hers tighter. 'You didn't know; he didn't ask you?'

'No. Well... What does it matter? You must have changed the name and entered it on Friday morning at the latest, before even asking me. I might have said no.'

'But you didn't.'

'That is not the point.'

'Josie, there is no point.' Turning her hand over in his,

he added, 'We are engaged; we are to be married in a couple of weeks. Accept the fact and let's eat.'

Josie was still seething with resentment as he virtually marched her into the pub with his hand at her elbow. She glanced around. It was a typical old coaching inn, all dark oak and low ceilings, a few oak tables and chairs, and along one wall were small dining alcoves. Not the sort of place she would have expected Conan to frequent. But hey! What did she know about pubs? She had a small circle of good friends she socialised with, and if they went for a drink it was usually to a wine bar in Cheltenham. Anyway, Josie wasn't much of a drinker—except at that fatal party, she thought bitterly.

'Sit down, Josie, and try to look less like you're being led to the gallows.' Conan urged her into a small banquette made for two and slid in beside her.

'Do you have to sit next to me?' she snapped. He was crowding her, his long leg resting against hers.

'In your present mood, yes,' he bit out. 'I wouldn't put it past you to run away.'

'Well, what do you expect? You had no right to put the announcement in the paper without telling me.'

'I had every right.' He turned sideways, his dark eyes narrowed on her mutinous face. 'Let's get one thing straight here and now.' His strong hand grasped hers and lifted it to within inches of her own face.

'See that ring? That gives me every right and don't you forget it.' His savage undertone sent icy fingers of fear walking up her rigid spine.

The gloves were off with a vengeance, Josie thought. The suave sophistication Conan portrayed to the world was a thin veneer to mask the ruthless predator beneath. 'We are not married yet,' she snorted inelegantly. But the glitter in his piercing dark eyes sent a shiver of apprehension through

her body. 'Engagements are easily broken,' she continued.
Why she was carrying on baiting him Josie did not know.

His grip on her hand tightened and she had to bite down
a whimper of pain. 'Not this one, lady,' Conan drawled
with silken emphasis on 'lady.' 'No one makes a fool out
of me.'

'You do that perfectly well for yourself!' Josie snapped
back. 'And let go of my hand.'

'Well, if it isn't Conan, my old mate.' A booming voice
interrupted their heated exchange.

Conan ignored her request and glanced across at the man
standing at the opposite side of the table.

'Bootsy!' he exclaimed. 'I might have guessed you
would still be drinking here.'

Josie looked at the short, red-haired, blue-eyed man who
had spoken and then back at Conan, and was surprised to
see a smile of genuine pleasure lighting up his rugged features.

'Not drinking… I own the place. But what about you? I
heard on the Beeches bush telegraph that you're about to
be married.' It was Josie's turn to get the full power of
twinkling blue eyes. 'And this must be the lucky lady. I
could tell you stories about this 'un you wouldn't believe.'
He nodded towards Conan.

'Oh. I'm sure I would,' Josie said dryly.

'Too late, Bootsy.' Conan's long arm curved around her
shoulders, and his dark head bent to nuzzle her neck. 'Behave yourself!' he whispered, his tongue flicking around
the inner whorls of her ear. His breath fanned her cheek as
he raised his head, and her heartbeat thundered in her ear-
drums. She couldn't have spoken even if she'd wanted to,
but Conan had no problem.

'Josie knows all my weak spots and then some,' Conan
favoured her with a long, lingering perusal, his dark eyes
roaming over her face and down to the firm swell of her

breasts beneath the fine red wool of her dress, then slowly back to her face. 'And I certainly know all of hers,' he opined with a sensual smile. 'Don't I, darling?' The other man was left in no doubt that they shared a very intimate relationship.

She wanted to slap Conan, but instead she snuggled under his arm. Two could play at that game, she thought furiously. 'He is so naughty,' she simpered, giving Bootsy a wide smile. 'But so romantic. Would you like to see my ring?' Conan had no choice but to let go of her hand. She held it out over the table. 'It was his grandmother's. Isn't that the most wildly romantic gift?' and, turning a sickly-sweet smile on Conan, she added, 'My hero.'

Bootsy shot an alarmed glance at Conan, then looked at Josie and tried to smile. 'Yes, well, very nice. Congratulations. Now, what can I get you to eat? The steak pie is perfect, but then everything I serve is perfect.'

Conan ordered for both of them and Bootsy could not get away fast enough.

'You realise, Josie, the man thinks I'm marrying a simpering idiot,' Conan said dryly.

'Serves you right,' She shrugged off his arm, but couldn't prevent a chuckle escaping her. 'He did look a bit shocked.' Her violet eyes sparkling with amusement clashed with Conan's, and for a moment they were in complete accord.

'Josie, you're a witch!' he said with wry amusement. 'But if this relationship is going to work,' he added, suddenly serious, 'we've both got to at least try to be civil to each other.'

'Yes, I know,' she conceded. 'But in future could you please ask me first before you arrange things?'

Surprisingly the evening turned out much better than Josie expected. Conan was a good conversationalist, the food was simple but perfectly cooked and they discussed music, books, and finally ended up having a heated debate over the best film ever made.

Josie said *Casablanca* and Conan insisted he liked *The Graduate* better.

'You can't be serious!' Josie cried. 'Bogart made a truly noble sacrifice for the woman he loved.'

'True, but personally I would leave nobility to the fool, and take the girl and run, as in *The Graduate*.'

'Somehow that doesn't surprise me.' She grinned, caught the predatory gleam in his eyes, and knew he was not joking.

They drove home a little after ten, and they parted on a sober note.

'Tomorrow, at the funeral, you won't do anything foolish,' Conan insisted as they walked up to the door. 'Like having hysterics or throwing yourself on the coffin.'

'No,' she said simply, tilting her head back to look up coldly into his shadowed face. 'I am well aware that to the world at large Charles was simply a friend to me, and the brother of my fiancé. Why do you think I went to work today? I am as capable as you are of playing my part in this marriage of convenience. You have nothing to worry about.' On that note she opened the door, and closed it behind her in his face.

The next day, in Beeches village church, Josie only half listened to the vicar's eulogy for Charles. The biological father of her child was being buried, and the tears on her cheeks were no more than she would have cried at any friend's funeral. Her feelings for Charles had been fleeting at best, and she felt swamped by guilt. She glanced sideways at her companion. Conan was dressed in a long black cashmere overcoat, a black suit beneath, black tie, the brilliant white of his shirt only serving to emphasise his sombre attire. His face was equally grave, and he stared impassively ahead, not a flicker of emotion on his granite features.

She shivered, and immediately his large hand found hers and squeezed her cold fingers.

'Not long now,' he murmured without turning his head.

However, the shiver had not been caused by emotion for Charles, but by a sudden realisation that she had agreed to share her life and unborn child with the man at her side. A man who looked like some dark fallen angel.

Later, at the graveside, when the six soldiers from Charles's regiment who had acted as pallbearers fired a salute, Josie nearly jumped out of her skin.

Only Conan's arm around her shoulder prevented her stumbling. 'Steady, Josie; you're doing fine.'

'No histrionics, you mean,' she whispered angrily.

He turned her into his arms, as if comforting her, and only Josie saw the wicked glint in his dark eyes as his arms held her trapped against him. 'Now, now, darling,' he said, drawling the endearment so the people beside them could hear. 'I know it's tragic, but I'm certain Charles wouldn't have wanted us to delay our wedding, because of his untimely death.'

'If you say so,' Josie agreed. She could not do much else, as Conan had so cleverly sown the seed of an early marriage among the mourners at the funeral without even trying.

'Not as bad as you thought, hmm?' Conan remarked as he drove the sleek BMW car the short journey to her home.

Her guilt at her own lack of deep feeling for Charles made her lash out at Conan. 'If burying your bother can be considered not bad, I suppose so,' she said witheringly.

'I forgot he was the love of your life. Right?' He shot her an angry glance as he stopped the car outside her house.

'Right,' she lied, and slid out of the car.

Conan did not bother getting out but simply said, 'I'll see you tomorrow,' and drove off in a squeal of tyres.

The next day was even worse. Josie sat at her desk, trying to read the document in front of her. Usually she enjoyed her job as a legal secretary, but with all that had happened in her life lately she was having trouble concentrating. It did not help at all when Conan strode into the office of Brownlow Solicitors as if he owned the place.

Josie jumped to her feet, knocking a coffee cup off the edge of her desk to the floor. 'What are you doing here?' she cried, her eyes skating over his long body casually dressed in blue jeans and a heavy navy blue sweater.

'Hello, darling.' He walked towards her and planted a brief kiss on her startled lips.

'What's going on?' A deep voice intruded as Mr Brownlow, the senior partner, walked in. 'Oh, Conan. Nice of you to call, but I hope you're not going to make a habit of distracting my secretary.'

'I certainly hope I am,' Conan quipped, and the two men shared a very masculine laugh.

Josie looked from one man to the other, and then at the floor to hide her angry colour. Spying the cup, she bent to pick it up, and, on straightening, caught the end of the conversation.

'I was in town on business, and thought I would check Josie had given you her notice. She's so excited, she can hardly remember her own name.' Conan placed an arm around her waist and hauled her hard against him.

'Of course the death of my brother has complicated things a bit. But the wedding is going ahead as arranged in just over two weeks time. It is unfortunate—I know how much Josie loves working here—but with my commitments in London and overseas, you can see it would be impossible for her to continue once we're married.'

Josie glanced wildly around the room. Zoe was sitting at

her desk opposite staring at Conan as though he were the only man on the planet. Mr Brownlow, usually the most reserved of men, was smiling broadly at Conan.

'Of course, old chap; that will be fine. We will be sorry to lose her, but I understand perfectly. A woman has to follow her husband.'

'Wait a minute,' Josie began, about to argue, but was stopped by Conan's fingers digging sharply into her side. She immediately tensed; his close proximity had that effect on her. Plus if he kept grabbing her to control her in this way, she thought furiously, she was going to end up black and blue.

'And I couldn't bear to be without her for even a day,' Conan said huskily, turning his head to smile down meltingly into her eyes, but Josie saw the warning in their glinting depths, and remained silent.

Anyway, what could she say? she thought sombrely. She had agreed to marry Conan; she was wearing his ring. She had made her choice and now she must live with it. She just wished he weren't so super-efficient at arranging everything.

She knew she should be thanking him, not trying to hinder him. But she felt as if she had been deposited on a rollercoaster ride against her will, and there was no stopping.

'Er, yes.' Mr Brownlow coughed. 'Well, back to work. Take an early lunch, Josie; you must have a lot to do.' And he went back to his own office.

Twenty minutes later, sitting opposite Conan in the local wine bar with a plate of spaghetti in front of her, she listened in tight-lipped anger as he outlined the details of the wedding.

'Is Beeches church okay with you?'

'Why can't we simply go to the registrar?' she demanded. 'Anyway you have to book the church weeks in advance.'

'All taken care of. I got a special licence and the vicar is quite happy.'

It took every bit of self-control she possessed not to tip the spaghetti over his arrogant head. He had done it again. He'd arranged everything without discussing it with her.

'Something wrong?' Conan asked as the silence between them lengthened.

'No, no, of course not.' What was the point in fighting with him? She had agreed to marry him; where and when was of little importance.

'Good, because I have to leave soon, and I won't be back until the day before the wedding. If you need to get in touch, here is my home phone number in London. But I'll give you a call anyway.'

When Conan finally left her at the entrance to her office, she heaved a sigh of relief. He was a puzzling, powerful, autocratic male, and it took all her energy simply to survive in his presence. How she would survive being married to him she did not dare dwell on.

A little over two weeks later Josie scrambled into the passenger seat of Conan's car and momentarily closed her eyes. The wedding was over, and right at this moment she didn't care what the future would bring.

'I think that went quite well,' Conan remarked as he slid in behind the driving wheel and put the key in the ignition.

'As farces go it was probably one of the best,' Josie muttered.

Conan's sharp dark eyes rested on her face. 'It is only a farce if you make it so, Josie. We can behave as mature, civilised adults, or—'

'You're right,' she cut in. 'Please just start the car.'

He half turned in his seat. 'Have I told you you look

beautiful today.' His dark eyes skimmed over her small
body, elegantly clothed in a pale blue designer suit. 'Mrs
Zarcourt.' Leaning forward, he brushed his lips lightly over
her own, before starting the car.

Josie raised startled eyes to his, and let herself really look
at him for the first time that day. His long body looked
powerful clad in a superb grey silk suit. His jet-black hair,
combed severely back from his broad forehead, only intensified the effect of his firmly chiselled profile. He was a
very attractive man and she had married him.

It was dark when the car stopped outside a tall three-
storeyed Georgian terrace house in the heart of Mayfair.
Conan urged her into the house with a hand in the centre
of her back, her suitcase in his other hand.

'Would you like a drink or something to eat?' he asked,
dropping her suitcase on the floor and straightening to his
full height, his dark eyes curiously impersonal on her small
face.

'No, thank you.' Josie was suddenly struck by an attack
of nerves. What had she done?

'Then perhaps a quick tour of the house?'

'Yes, yes.' They were talking like two complete strangers, Josie thought, and almost laughed.

But she lost all trace of humour when he showed her into
the master bedroom.

'You look tired,' Conan murmured clasping her shoulders in his large hands. She stiffened her back ramrod-
straight, and glanced warily up into his hard face. 'Get
ready for bed and I'll be back in ten minutes with a hot
drink for you.'

A hot drink, and what else? Josie glanced around the
room. There was only one bed...

'My bed is next door in the dressing room,' Conan said
dryly, accurately reading her thoughts. 'You have nothing
to fear.'

*   *   *

The following morning the smell of ground coffee led Josie downstairs to the kitchen. Conan was standing by the counter, a box of cornflakes in his hand. 'Good morning, Josie. I didn't expect you so early.' He smiled, and she gave him a cool smile back. 'Would you like some breakfast?'

'You make your own?' she asked, surprised. 'I thought you'd have a housekeeper.'

'I do—Jeffrey. He arrives at nine and leaves at six, and nothing I say will persuade him to live in.'

'Well, let me make your breakfast,' she offered, walking across the room to where he stood. 'I always did for my father.'

'I'm not your father.' He stared down at her, an enigmatic expression on his dark face.

'I know, but I am a good cook,' she said firmly. She was determined to assert herself from the beginning and preserve a formal but polite relationship between them.

'Yes, okay. At least that's one wifely duty you can perform.'

She glanced suspiciously at him. What kind of crack was that? But he gave her a bland smile and sat down at the table. She could feel his eyes following her around as she searched the cupboards and prepared ham and eggs.

After breakfast Conan insisted on taking her out. To 'sort her out', as he put it. He registered her with his doctor in Harley Street, at the same time booking her into a private clinic for the birth of the baby. Any objections she made he quickly overruled. According to the doctor the baby was due in the middle of May.

On returning home in the evening, they were met in the hall by Jeffrey, who had prepared a celebratory meal for them. Josie liked the white-haired old man immediately. But dining alone with Conan was a fraught affair. He said very little, and immediately when they were finished he retired to his study.

A few weeks later Josie pushed her way on to the tube and heaved a sigh of relief. She had spent longer shopping than she had intended to, but finally in a small boutique she had found the perfect creation for herself—an exquisite dress in floating chiffon that cunningly disguised her thickening waistline.

She got off the tube and walked along the pavement towards the house she now called home, thinking of how her life had changed in the past weeks. There was a lot to be said for being a lady of leisure. She had visited all the museums, and quite a few art galleries. As for Conan, she didn't actually spend much time with him.

In the mornings she made breakfast for both of them before Jeffrey arrived. Conan went to the office for the day and usually at night they shared dinner together and talked about their respective day. Then Conan went to his study and Josie went to bed. It was all very civilised, and if sometimes Josie imagined there was something more in his penetrating gaze, and the way he would drop a soft kiss on her cheek for no reason, she dismissed the notion as a combination of her over-active imagination and the peculiar tension she appeared to suffer from when she spent any length of time in his company.

The weekends were not much different. Conan, it seemed, was a workaholic, as well as being the most even-tempered man she had ever met; he was always coolly polite and that suited Josie just fine. She had had enough trauma to last her a lifetime.

Balancing her parcels in one hand, she inserted the key in the front door, but before she could turn it the door swung open and she was dragged unceremoniously into the hall by Conan's large hand manacled around her arm.

'Where the hell have you been?' he snarled, giving her such a shock that she dropped all her parcels on the floor.

'Look what you've made me do!' she exclaimed, eyeing her scattered purchases. 'Thank heaven there's nothing breakable.'

'Nothing breakable!' he gritted between clenched teeth. 'You're lucky I don't break your lovely neck. Do you realise what time it is? Do you?'

Josie lifted her head, her eyes widening in surprise as she met the full force of his angry gaze. He was absolutely furious. 'It's only about eight,' she retorted. And here she had just been telling herself that Conan was the most even-tempered of men. She had certainly got that wrong if the look on his face was anything to go by! Warily she took a step back to put some space between them.

'Only eight! Are you mad? I was just about to call the police!'

'I'm sorry, but the tube was crowded,' she said, though not convinced he deserved an apology.

'The tube!' he snarled. 'Is there no end to your stupidity?'

'I am not stupid!' she shot back. 'I was simply shopping.'

'Don't take me for a fool, Josie. Unlike America, in England the stores close at six.'

'Not all stores,' she cried, her temper rising at his high-handed attitude. He had no right to question her. 'For *your* information,' she added scathingly, 'I went to buy a dress— for *your* dinner party tomorrow night. Satisfied?'

'Satisfied,' he snarled, and he grasped her hand in his much larger one, dragging her further into the hall.

She winced and stumbled against him. 'Please, you're hurting my wrist.' As her plea registered he dropped her hand as if it were a hot potato.

'Hurting you!' he exclaimed incredulously. 'You don't

know the meaning of the word. I've been hurting since the first day I set eyes on you.' And, keeping a tight hold on her arm, he urged her through the open study door, growling, 'What I have to say to you is best said in private.'

Josie had no time to reflect on his strange comment as she noticed Jeffrey at the end of the hall. Funny; he should have gone home long ago. Maybe that was why Conan was making such a fuss—on Jeffrey's behalf. But eight o'clock was hardly the middle of the night, Josie thought rebelliously. But she had no more time to think as Conan pushed her into a leather armchair.

'Sit there and listen, child,' he commanded.

'I am not a child,' she denied angrily.

'Then stop behaving like one,' Conan growled. Then he proceeded to treat her to a tirade, the ferociousness of which she would never have believed he was capable of. Too stunned to move or respond, she watched him pace back and forth in front of her like some wild jungle beast in search of prey. He called her every idiot under the sun and then some, without stopping for breath. His jacket and tie had been discarded long since and, mesmerised, she thought how magnificent he looked. His white silk shirt hung half open, revealing his broad tanned chest, matted with curls that arrowed down out of sight, and his grey pleated trousers tantalisingly traced the hard contours of his thighs. He exuded an aura of powerful male sexuality that was frightening but fascinating in its intensity.

For weeks Josie had convinced herself that Conan was satisfied with their pleasantly polite relationship, upholding their original agreement to the letter. But now she was not so sure, as she realised how utterly ruthless he could be when roused. She tensed angrily under the lash of his tongue, but inexplicably her anger drained away to be replaced by a different passion. Her pulse rate accelerated as her eyes slid over the whole length of him to rest on his custom-made leather shoes. She was too afraid to look up as wryly she acknowledged her fear was based more on her own reaction to his vibrant brand of sexuality than the words he roared at her. She needed to get away, and quick…

'And look at me when I am talking to you!' he commanded furiously. Stopping directly in front of her, and leaning over her, he placed a huge hand on either arm of the chair, effectively blocking her escape.

Warily Josie raised her eyes to his, struck by the banked-down fury in his gaze.

'That's better,' he intoned with a silky softness that frightened her more than his shouting had done. 'Now, little girl, I think it's time you and I got a few things straight. You're not in the Cotswolds now, but in the heart of a big city, and for starters you will never go out or stay out late without informing Jeffrey or myself where you are. Is that understood?' he demanded forcefully.

Josie's eyes clung to his handsome face, incapable of breaking the contact, trapped by the power of his personality as much as his large body towering over her. She sank deeper into the seat. His closeness was having a strange effect on her. She swallowed hard, and deep down inside her an unfamiliar ache unfurled. An ache to feel the strength of his arms around her, his hard mouth on hers, and how had she never noticed before the thick, curling dark lashes that shielded his glittering eyes?

'Do you understand me, Josie?' he reiterated.

She jumped. 'Yes, yes, I understand.'

'You're sure?' His dark eyes gleamed golden as he held her gaze, and for a long, tense moment they simply stared at each other.

'We struck a bargain, you and I,' Conan drawled with ruthless inflexibility. 'A name, and a father for your child.' His eyes did not leave hers for a second. 'In return I eventually get what I want. But I will not put up with your callous disregard for the concern of Jeffrey, or myself, towards you and the baby. Understood?'

'Yes. I know, I'm not a fool, I can hear you,' she said curtly. 'Probably half the street can hear you. No going out without telling you. Oh, jailer!' she ended defiantly.

His eyes flared angrily. 'If I was your jailer, do you really think I would have allowed you to run around London on your own?'

'No.' Josie knew she was being unfair, and suddenly feeling very tired, and in no mood to argue, she added, 'And I will apologise to Jeffrey in the morning. I never thought he would stay behind.'

As if sensing her exhaustion, Conan straightened up and, taking a deep breath, expelled it slowly. 'And I'm sorry for shouting at you, Josie, but you have no idea how worried I was to arrive home at six and find you hadn't yet arrived. I couldn't imagine what had happened to you, and poor Jeffrey was worried sick. He refused to leave until you returned. Promise you will never, ever give me a shock like that again?'

At his words Josie felt the beginnings of a strange warmth building inside her. Conan had been worried about her. Why the thought should please her she did not question; she only knew it did.

'I didn't mean to worry you, Conan, but I had nothing to wear for tomorrow night. I had to buy a dress.'

'Ah, the age-old female cry: "I have nothing to wear!" I should have guessed,' he drawled, a very masculine grin lighting his dark face. 'The very least you can do is go and put it on and let me see why my dinner has been delayed for so long.' Reaching down, he took her hand and pulled her to her feet. 'But make it snappy, hmm?'

Josie picked up her parcels from the hall and shot upstairs. Shedding her clothes, she speedily unwrapped her new dress, and slipped it over her head. Tiny shoe-string straps supported the bodice that skimmed the soft curves of her breasts; empire-style, the skirt fell from beneath her breasts, skimming her hips to end in soft folds at her feet. Coloured from the palest pink through lavender to the deepest blue, it enhanced her pale complexion, emphasising the violet of her eyes.

She sighed, if only she were taller. And, hastily finding her only pair of four-inch-heeled sandals she slipped them on.

Conan was in the hall as she glided down the staircase. She must have made some sound, because he turned and stared up at her. His dark eyes narrowed intently on her delicate frame. She stopped a few steps from the bottom, paralysed by the intensity of his gaze as silently his eyes swept slowly over her, in a slow, sexy scrutiny that brought colour to her cheeks.

'Well, what do you think?' she asked, her glance colliding with his, her colour increasing at the sensuous gleam in his eyes. What was happening to her? She had thought after her disastrous affair with Charles that she was probably frigid. But the longer she spent with Conan, the more she doubted herself. Tonight she was achingly aware of him. Swiftly she lowered her lashes, terrified he would recognise how he was affecting her.

'You look beautiful, Josie,' he drawled throatily. 'Absolutely perfect.'

She took the next few steps in a hurry, flustered by his compliment. She felt her ankle turn. 'Damn these heels,' she muttered darkly.

'Careful,' Conan husked, folding her in his arms to steady her. 'Should you be wearing high heels in your condition?' he asked.

'Probably not,' she admitted ruefully, slipping her feet out of the sandals, her small hands clasping his broad shoulders to steady herself. 'But I'm vain.' She lifted laughing eyes to his face, and that was her mistake.

Conan's head bent, his lips brushing softly over her mouth in a gentle kiss, and the warmth of his mouth ignited an immediate response in her firm young body. The tension she'd felt when he'd held her before had mysteriously vanished. Instead she relaxed against him, her fingers sliding along his broad shoulders to lace through the thick black hair of his head, her lips parting invitingly under his. Then she was clinging to him, every part of her moulded against his large body. Her heart pounded in her breast as his tongue expertly searched the moist dark interior of her mouth, colliding and sliding with hers in wickedly seductive passion.

The blood roared in her head, blanking out all thought of resistance. The fierce pressure of his strong arms around her slender body was a delightful pain. Gradually he broke the kiss, his almost black eyes burning down into hers. Then, slowly, teasingly, he moved his hips against her, making her vitally aware of his own state of arousal in the process. But still he held her, which was just as well from Josie's point of view; she doubted she could have stood by herself.

She should have been frightened, but for some reason she wasn't. Her legs felt like rubber and she was incapable of speech. She stared mutely up at him, her violet eyes unknowingly inviting him to continue, and he did. His mouth once again found hers, and eagerly she gave in to the wonder of his kiss yet again.

'Well, Josie, that was nice,' he opined softly, lifting her hands from his shoulders and easing her away from him. 'But I think you'd better run along and get changed or I might be tempted to forget all about dinner.' He chuckled.

Conan's soft laugh broke through her dazed senses. Dinner-Jeffrey-reality intruded like a douche of cold water. Picking up her sandals, she fled upstairs, as if all the hounds in hell were after her, and Conan's mocking laughter ringing in her ears did not help.

'That was nice,' Conan had said. Nice? It was incredible. Josie had never thought a couple of kisses could arouse such a tumult of emotions. To her it had been earth-shattering, and she was mortified at her own reaction. But by the time she had changed her dress for a simple black sweater and plaid skirt she had almost convinced herself it had been an apparition on her part—maybe just her raging hormones caused by her pregnancy. Although her innate honesty forced her to admit she had been battling her attraction to Conan ever since the night of the party. As for her pregnancy, it had been remarkably trouble-free so far— no sickness, nothing except an expanding waistline.

Walking back downstairs, she headed for the kitchen. To her surprise Conan was setting the pine scrubbed table with dishes and cutlery. He looked up as she closed the door behind her.

'Good; that was quick. I was thinking of starting without you—I'm starving.' Turning to the cooker, he said over his shoulder, 'Jeffrey has left my favourite—a steak and ale casserole with dumplings. Sit down and we'll eat.'

Pulling up a chair, Josie did as she was told. If she had imagined the kiss would change anything between them, his prosaic statement had quickly disillusioned her. She watched him through her lowered lashes as he bent over the oven, his firmly moulded buttocks and long legs beautifully defined by the taut fabric of his trousers. She grew hot with embarrassment as she realised where her thoughts were leading, and hastily looked away.

She had not known it was possible to be so sexually aware of a man. Her palms were damp and she had to fight to control her erratic heartbeat. She grimaced; it was plain to see that Conan didn't have the same problem as he turned around and placed a large casserole dish in the middle of the table.

'You must be hungry after the busy day you've had. I know I am.' Flashing her a quick grin, he served himself a huge helping of stew and started to eat.

Josie was surprised to discover that despite her turbulent emotions she was incredibly hungry. By the time she had devoured a healthy portion of dinner, and Conan asked her if she wanted more coffee, she had managed to suppress her wayward emotions altogether. 'No, thanks, this is enough for me,' she said, and she even managed a cool smile.

'You're getting over your grief, I think,' Conan said softly into the silence.

'Oh, yes.' Fed and relaxed, she had never felt better. 'Yes, indeed.' She smiled at him, then immediately felt horribly guilty. She should not have agreed so readily; after all, it was Conan's half-brother who had died. In an attempt to justify herself she continued, 'I didn't know...well, I mean...I didn't go out with Charles for very long...' She trailed off; she was only making it worse. She caught the glint of anger in his dark eyes, and wished she had never tried to explain. But surprisingly Conan smiled.

'Don't worry; there's no need to feel guilty, Josie.'

She felt the colour rise in her cheeks, and could not meet his eyes. Dear heaven! How could he read her mind so easily? she wondered.

'I knew Charles a lot better than you. And he wouldn't have wanted you to grieve for ever.' Levering himself out of the chair, he crossed to her side. 'You're tired,' he said, and reaching for her hand, he pulled her to her feet.

Josie swayed slightly; it had been a long day. 'Yes, I am.' She yawned.

Conan steadied her with an arm around her shoulders and led her to the door. 'It's bedtime for you, my girl.' He pressed a swift kiss on her softly parted lips, his dark eyes smiling down into hers.

With the taste of him on her lips, her bemused gaze clung to his and for the first time since their marriage she allowed herself to think that maybe it would not be such a bad idea if their convenient arrangement matured into a sexual relationship. Conan had kissed her and obviously cared about her; his reaction when she was late surely proved as much. Maybe she was not as frigid as she thought—around Conan she was anything but cold. Involuntarily she raised her fingers to her lips, as though to capture his last kiss.

'Bed, Josie,' he reminded her, chuckling at her reaction.

She dashed upstairs and her last thought before sleep claimed her was, If only she was his girl...

The following morning, there was a spring in her step and a sparkle in her eyes that she was totally unaware of. When Conan walked into the kitchen she had already made the coffee and was about to start cooking ham and eggs. She flashed him a brilliant smile. 'Good morning.'

'Is it?' he demanded and, crossing over to the stove, he took the pan she was holding out of her hand, put it down on the bench, slipped his arms around her waist and turned her into the circle of his arms.

His dark eyes glinted golden in the early morning light as he searched her upturned face with slow deliberation, his gaze lingering on the lush bow of her mouth. She breathed the clean male scent of him, felt the enveloping warmth of his large body. Then his head descended very slowly, giving her all the time in the world to stop him if she wanted to. Instead she shivered as his lips sought hers, the pulse beating rapidly in the side of her neck. A low moan escaped her and he raised his head, his mouth swallowing her groan.

Her heart leapt in her breast as his teeth gently nipped her bottom lip, his tongue erotically stroking hers. Her body softened and arched slightly in his embrace and her breasts felt swollen and aching in contact with his broad chest. When he gently released her she was sure he must be aware of the startling effect he had on her. But he did not show it.

'You're right. It is a good morning, Josie—the best ever.' His eyes, glinting with masculine satisfaction, held her own. 'But don't bother cooking for me; I'll just have coffee. I want to save myself for tonight.'

Was he dieting? Or was it some other appetite he was alluding to? Bemused, she poured his coffee in a daze, and watched him drink it and leave. Long after he had gone her lips still tingled from his brief parting kiss...

Jeffrey's arrival broke through her daydreaming, and together they began preparing for the evening's dinner party. Between them they had decided on a menu of fresh vegetable soup, followed by beef Wellington with all the trimmings and a Grand Marnier soufflé for dessert. Suddenly Josie was really looking forward to meeting some of Conan's friends and she wanted everything to be perfect.

By midday everything was prepared that could be prepared in advance. Satisfied with her morning's work, Josie ran lightly upstairs to the master bedroom, sighing contentedly. She loved the room; an imp of mischief had her adding to herself that all it needed was for Conan to share the huge bed with her instead of sleeping in the dressing room. Blushing at her wayward thoughts, she bent down to pick up the sandals she had dropped on the floor last night.

Then disaster struck. One of the straps was broken. 'Damn', she muttered, turning the offending sandal over in her hand. They were the only shoes she possessed that were suitable to wear with an evening gown. Glancing at the bedside clock, she groaned out loud. If she hurried perhaps she would have time to go and buy a new pair.

Quickly slipping into the blue suit she had worn for her wedding, she ran downstairs. Jeffrey was standing in the hall replacing the telephone receiver, but before she could speak he solved the problem for her.

'That was Mr Zarcourt. He left some papers he needs today in the study so I'm going to drop them off at his office.'

'Oh, good, I'll go with you, and we can make a detour, because I need some new shoes.' She grinned. 'You don't mind, do you, Jeffrey?'

'Well, no—as long as you're quick,' he responded gruffly but Josie knew he didn't mind.

The taxi drew to a halt outside an impressive-looking building in the heart of the city on Moorgate. Josie looked around with interest; she had never been to Conan's bank before. Clutching her purse, she was about to follow Jeffrey out of the taxi, when a man on the opposite side of the road caught her eye. She sank back into the seat.

It was Conan, not ten yards away. She saw his strong profile, his thick black hair gleaming in the December sunlight, and as she watched she saw the blonde run up to him and fling her arms around him. She saw them kiss. Josie even thought she heard the sound of his laughter as he stepped back and tucked the woman's hand through his arm. And walked away.

'I won't be long,' Jeffrey told her.

'Okay.' Josie's gaze was fixed on the couple strolling down the street. Conan was tall, but his companion was almost as big. A very beautiful blonde, she was all long legs, mini-skirt, and lush curves. Was that the kind of woman Conan liked?

Josie watched until they disappeared from sight, her whole body clenched in pain. She laid her head back against the seat and closed her eyes, but nothing could shut out the image of Conan and the woman. She felt as though her heart had been split in two, her hands clenched into fists, her nails digging into her palms as she forced herself to breathe slowly and deeply, fighting down the tears she ached to cry.

'Are you all right, miss?'

The cab driver's voice broke into her anguished thoughts. 'Yes, yes, I'm fine,' she said, slowly opening her eyes. She was aware of the worried look on the driver's face. 'A touch of indigestion,' she murmured. The lie worked; with a nod, the man turned back to the front.

How stupid she had been, how blind. Of course a handsome, successful man like Conan would have a woman; he was not the type to be celibate. She had realised as much the day he had proposed marriage and she'd asked him about his women. So, now that she knew he had a lady friend, why was it causing her so much pain?

She had always known the reason Conan had married her. He had been perfectly honest about it. He wanted Beeches Manor back from his father, and marrying Josie had been his way of getting it. True, they had managed to live together civilly over the past weeks, but surely she had not been imagining there could ever be anything more between them? She groaned in self-disgust, forced to admit to herself that maybe she had...

But now the blinkers had been torn from her eyes, and Josie wanted to scream at fate for doing this to her. It was jealousy, pure unadulterated jealousy, vicious in its pain, that was causing her such anguish. She was in love with Conan.

It was no good blaming fate; it was entirely her own stupid fault. Theirs was a marriage of convenience. What had Conan said when she had asked him about fidelity? 'You can count on my fidelity as much as I can count on yours.' Given that she was carrying another man's child, that gave Conan plenty of leeway...

'Where to now, Mrs Zarcourt?' Jeffrey demanded, sliding into the car beside her.

Mrs Zarcourt! But for how long? Until the child was born, or Major Zarcourt died? Josie did not know... She named a well-known shoe store, forcing her mind back to the present.

Later Josie lay across the bed, tears slowly drying on her cheeks. This was no good, she admonished herself sternly; the last thing she needed was to meet their dinner guests with red-rimmed eyes. She had told Jeffrey she needed a rest on their return from the city, and had come straight upstairs. It had been an excuse... She was hiding. It was that simple.

But not any more. She had made a bargain and would stick to it. She slid her legs over the side of the bed and stood up. She would have to face Conan some time, and she might look marginally better if she slapped on some make-up. She took a quick shower and washed her hair. Then, seated at the dressing table wearing only her briefs, she eyed the tangled mass of wet black ringlets falling around her shoulders with disgust. Picking up the hairdryer she plugged it in and made an attempt to bring her hair into some kind of order.

But her concentration was shot... She had fallen in love with her husband, and he must never know... A hollow laugh escaped her at the irony of the situation. Heaven help her! She had to be the one girl in the world Conan could never love. Hadn't he seen her the night of the party, naked in the bed she had shared with his half-brother? Even now the shame of it made her burn with embarrassment.

Putting the hairdryer down, she studied her flushed reflection in the mirror—the small scrubbed face surrounded by a wild mass of curls, the small straight nose and full mouth all added up to a child, she thought bitterly. Worse! She had been behaving like the child Conan had called her.

This morning his parting kiss had compounded the illusion in her mind from the previous night that their relationship was shifting to that of lovers. She had not examined her feelings at the time but now she was forced to recognise her own wholehearted response to Conan's kisses and the mood of euphoria she had felt at the prospect of a deepening relationship between them.

Josie sighed, her violet eyes shadowed in pain. How wrong she had been, she thought bitterly. Yet she could not blame Conan; it was not his fault. He had given her time and space to help her get over the grief he imagined she must feel at the death of Charles. Guilt swamped her as she finally admitted the truth to herself. The death of Charles had not worried her half as much as finding out she was pregnant.

Straightening her shoulders, she picked up a brush, and dragged it through her tangled hair. It was time she got dressed. Sitting thinking what a complete and utter mess she had made of her life was not going to help her or her child. As for tonight, it was up to her to play the part of the perfect wife for Conan in front of his friends, without him ever finding out she had been foolish enough to fall in love with him.

'Not ready yet, Josie? You'd better hurry up; our guests will be arriving shortly.' Conan's deep-voiced command echoed in the silence of the room.

CHAPTER FOUR

JOSIE spun around on the chair, the brush dropping from her hand. 'I didn't hear you come in!' she exclaimed, her eyes flying to Conan, who was standing just inside the room.

Her startled gaze roamed over him. He had removed his tie and the jacket of his suit and the first few buttons of his shirt were open, exposing the tanned flesh. His black hair fell forward over his forehead, ruffled as though he had been running his fingers through it. He looked tired, but his firm lips were enticingly sensuous, and his eyes... Her own were captured and held by the brilliant gleam of male appreciation she saw lurking in their depths.

She watched as he walked towards her. It was only when he reached out a hand to her that she came to her senses and remembered she was virtually naked.

Hastily she dropped her head and folded her arms defensively over her bare breasts. His hand closed around her arm, and she trembled as he urged her to her feet.

'Why so modest, Josie? I have seen you naked before,' he reminded her, and, gently unfolding her arms, he held them at her sides. 'I don't want you to be embarrassed with me. I am your husband, and I thought last night we were finally making some progress.' His dark gaze dropped to her firm breasts. 'I hope I wasn't wrong,' he opined huskily.

Colour flooded her cheeks and she was helpless to control the burgeoning awareness of her rose-tipped nipples to his hungry gaze. She had not known that she was so incredibly sensitive there; only a look and she ached. But with the ache came anger.

Wrong, he had said! It was Josie who had got it wrong, that was for sure. His dishevelled state probably had more to do with the blonde he had spent the afternoon with than hard work, and that thought gave her the strength to respond.

'I don't know what you're talking about,' she denied curtly, to some point over his left shoulder. It was dreadful. How could she hope to hide her love from him when every nerve in her body leapt to life at the sight of him? But she had to... Charles had caused her pain, but she knew it was nothing to the agony she would suffer if Conan ever discovered she had been stupid enough to fall in love with him.

'Are you sure you're okay?' His query broke into her troubled thoughts. 'You haven't heard a word I've said. I thought you were getting over your habit of daydreaming.'

If only he knew... She tilted her head back and forced herself to look at him. Then she wished she hadn't, as his arms slipped around her waist and she found herself held close against him, her nipples taut in contact with his chest.

'I do not daydream,' she contradicted him. 'I was tired, but I'm all right now.' And, wriggling out of his arms, she crossed to the bed and picked up her robe. She slipped it on and, tying the belt firmly around her waist, she made herself turn around to face him, adding, 'I went shopping this afternoon, so I thought I'd better rest before the party.'

'Jeffrey told me. It was a shame I missed you,' Conan offered, following her across the room. 'But I had a business lunch I couldn't avoid.'

Business? Was that what he called it? Some business... Josie thought angrily, and unconsciously took a step back.

Conan noted her withdrawal with a raised eyebrow, but continued talking. 'Angela Deacon from the New York office arrived this morning with some information I needed.'

He ran one hand distractedly through his hair and said. 'I've had a hell of a day.'

With e-mail, fax and the Internet at his disposal, she found his explanation a bit thin. But, clutching at straws, Josie considered maybe she had jumped to the wrong conclusion; maybe the woman was just a work colleague; maybe the kiss had been a simple welcome-back gesture. The thought was enough to deter her from arguing with him.

'It's all right, Conan. I understand and I didn't have much time anyway.' Catching sight of the bedside clock, she remarked, 'And I don't know if I want to be ready before our guests arrive.'

'You're not worried about this evening?' He eyed her quizzically.

'No, of course not. I have arranged dinner parties before—my father and I weren't complete recluses. I won't embarrass you; you needn't worry,' she told him briskly, her temper rising yet again. She knew he thought of her as a child but surely he wasn't ashamed of her as well?

'Josie, I didn't mean to suggest you weren't capable, but meeting people for the first time is a strain for anyone. But I want you to know I have complete faith in you, and I'm sure tonight will be a great success.'

'Condescending swine,' Josie murmured under her breath, and for an awful moment she thought she had spoken out loud. His dark eyes narrowed on her flushed face, and then, stepping forward, he bent his head and kissed the tip of her nose.

'I'd better go and dress, or neither of us will be ready in time.'

Shortly after, Josie descended the staircase to the hall. She knew she looked good. She had piled her hair on top of her head in a coronet of curls, held in place with diamanté combs. She had taken time over her make-up, and, wearing her new dress and shoes, her mirror had told her she had never looked better. Even so she took a deep breath before entering the drawing room.

Her heart missed a beat and she stopped inside the door. Conan was standing in profile, looking out of the window, a glass of whisky in his hand. The perfectly tailored black dinner suit and the crisp white of his shirt lifted his chiselled features from handsome to devastating. For a long moment Josie simply stared. But she must have made a sound because he half turned.

'Josie.' He said her name, his lips curling back over even white teeth in an appreciative smile as he walked across the room to her. 'You look exquisite,' he drawled softly, taking her hand in his.

'Thank you,' she said coolly, but his obvious delight in her appearance gave her confidence a much needed boost. Even though it was obvious he preferred big blondes...

'So polite,' he chuckled, and clasped her hand tightly. 'You know what you remind me of? When I was a small boy, every Christmas at the Manor we used to have a huge Christmas tree standing in the hall, and on the top a beautiful porcelain angel doll. I used to think it was so ethereal I ached to touch it, to keep it,' he murmured almost to himself, and, lifting his hand, he trailed one finger down her cheek.

His touch burnt like a trail of fire on Josie's soft skin, and it took all her will-power to fight down the tremor snaking through her body. With his other hand, he gently rubbed his thumb back and forward over her palm, and it suddenly occurred to Josie that her fierce reaction to Conan over the last couple of days was being heightened by his own changed attitude. The deliberate seductive touches, the passionate kisses... Oh, he had kissed her since the wedding, but usually a peck on the cheek, a supporting arm.

So why was he being so blatantly provocative with her now? Or was it her?

'I suppose that's a compliment—being likened to an angel—but I'm not sure I'm flattered at being called a doll,' she managed to say lightly. Conan stared down into her smiling eyes, his own expression unfathomable to Josie. The air around them seemed to crackle with an electric tension. She swallowed nervously; was she the only one aware of it?

'I was wrong; no doll could compare. You are beautiful. So very beautiful,' he repeated, the words a husky whisper as his head bent.

He was going to kiss her again and Josie's lips parted in helpless invitation. The ringing of the doorbell snapped her back to her senses, and, as she turned her head, his lips brushed her cheek.

'I will have to see the angel one day—it must be really something,' she babbled, hardly knowing what she was saying. Conan straightened, a brooding look passing over his rugged features.

'You can't. Charles smashed it.' And, dropping her hand, he brushed past her and into the hall to welcome their guests.

Josie followed him, the mention of Charles bringing her back to reality with a thump.

Jeffrey was ushering four people into the hall, and with a broad smile Conan caught Josie's hand again and made the introductions.

'Joe Smales, my personal manager, and his wife Betty.'

Josie smiled and said the appropriate words. They were a couple in their fifties, both large and jolly and eminently well suited, she thought, as were the next couple.

'And this is Harold Banes and his lovely wife Pamela, my surrogate mother.'

Josie was surprised by his comment and the warmth in

Conan's smile for the tiny woman in front of him. But he was right—Pamela was very lovely: forty-something, and even smaller than Josie, with a gamine face and bright red hair. Josie liked the older woman immediately when she said, 'At last! A woman almost as small as I am!'

Conan, the perfect host, guided everyone into the drawing room, and Jeffrey dispensed the drinks while the conversation flowed easily.

Josie sat back in her chair, nursing an orange juice, and listened to the quick repartee between the couples. It was obvious they were all good friends, and she began to relax and confidently join in the chat.

Everyone had been invited for seven-thirty to eat at eight. It was five to eight when the last couple arrived and the small ray of hope that had dwelt in Josie's heart since Conan's explanation of his lunch date was killed stone-dead.

Angela Deacon stalked in like some prima donna. Josie had gone into the hall to welcome her, and wished she hadn't. The woman made her feel like a midget.

'Ah, you must be Conan's little wife. How cute.' Sliding a mink coat off her shoulders, she swept past Josie.

Close up, the woman was stunning. Almost dressed in a wisp of black silk, with a neckline that plunged to her waist, the skirt moulded so tightly to her thighs it was a wonder she could walk—or so it appeared to Josie.

The man following Angela gave Josie some hope for a moment. He was tall, blond and handsome—but the hope was quickly squashed as he introduced himself as Steve, Angela's brother.

To Josie's formal request to take her coat, the stunning blonde replied, 'No, please join your guests. I know my way around Conan's house better than my own. I lived here for quite a while.' With that bombshell Angela sauntered upstairs, trailing the mink behind her.

The colour drained from Josie's face; she couldn't help it. She turned her stricken gaze on Conan, but he was engrossed in conversation with Steve, a smile on his handsome face. He had some nerve, Josie thought vehemently. The lying swine had said he had never lived with a woman...

The dinner was a nightmare for Josie. Angela seated herself on the right-hand side of Conan, and ignored everyone else present. Conan, with his wit and charm, kept the conversational ball rolling, but to Josie, seated at the opposite end of the table, it was apparent that her husband and Angela were much more than business colleagues. Conan smiled at the blonde with such indulgence that Josie felt like throttling him.

Afterwards she could not remember a word that had been spoken. Occasionally Conan caught her eye and gave her a reassuring smile, playing the part of the loving husband for the benefit of their guests. But finally the hypocrisy of it was too much for Josie, and she abruptly left the table, explaining that Jeffrey was leaving and she would serve the coffee in the drawing room. Her own fury surprised her. She did not consider herself a fiery person, but seeing Conan with Angela aroused a host of seething emotions she did not want to face.

On entering the room with a loaded tray ten minutes later, she almost dropped the lot on seeing Conan and Angela seated together on a sofa, so close it would have been hard to squeeze a pin between them. Pamela, as if sensing Josie's feelings jumped up and offered to help serve the coffee, and afterwards she insisted Josie sit down beside her.

'Don't let it worry you. We all know Angela of old,' she said in a quiet aside.

'Is it that obvious?' Josie asked with a wry grin. She had thought she had hidden her jealousy rather well.

'No, only to me, but then I have been watching you all evening.'

Josie stiffened. She had hoped Pamela might turn out to be her friend, but now she wasn't so sure.

'Don't get me wrong,' Pamela continued. 'I mean it in the nicest possible way. Conan is a particular friend of my husband and I. When he first came to London, he stayed with us. He is like the son I never had, and I wanted to make sure the girl he had married was right for him.' Taking Josie's hand in hers, she said, 'I am convinced you're just what he needs. You do love him?'

Josie felt the colour rise in her cheeks, but didn't deny it.

'It's all right. I can see you do, and I'm glad. Conan is a very guarded, private person, but that's not surprising when you consider his upbringing. It was bleak.'

'I gathered as much,' Josie mumbled.

'He has a great capacity for love, I'm sure. But there has never been anyone to love him,' Pamela said softly.

'Angela is more than willing by the look of it,' Josie offered cynically.

'Ah, the lovely Angela. Don't let her fool you. She has a brilliant brain, but no talent at all in her personal relationships.'

Watching Angela smiling into Conan's eyes, all breasts and thighs, Josie found it hard to believe and said as much.

'You're wrong. Conan has known Angela for ten years; her brother, Steve, is a very good friend of his. Conan has seen Angela through three divorces, and between each marriage she has made a play for him. But I'm happy to say he's far too clever to fall for her very obvious charms.'

Josie stifled a gasp. 'Three divorces? She doesn't look old enough,' she whispered.

'She is; she's a year older than Steve and Conan.'

'Come on, Pamela, you're hogging our hostess.' Mr

Smales's loud voice cut across their conversation, and then he proceeded to tell a very intricate shaggy-dog story about an Irishman and a brothel, until his wife stopped him and insisted it was time they left.

Josie breathed a sigh of relief when the last guest departed, the last one being Angela, of course. Josie turned to the stairs, her shoulders drooped and she felt about a hundred years old. Her one consolation was the clever cut of her dress meant no one had realised she was pregnant. So she was spared the humiliation of Angela knowing the real reason why Conan had married her. But for how long?

'Wait, Josie,' Conan demanded, and, locking the front door, he strode towards her.

She stopped, one foot on the stair, and looked up at him. 'I'm going to bed,' she said flatly. She didn't feel up to talking to him. It must have been obvious to everyone present that evening where his real feelings lay, irrespective of what Pamela had said.

Angela's parting shot as she left still rang in Josie's ears. 'I don't know how you tricked Conan into marrying you. Obviously I stayed away too long, but now I'm back you'd better get used to spending your evenings alone, sweetie.' Josie had been stunned by the malice in the older woman's eyes.

'Not so fast, Josie.' Conan's hand on her back stopped her departure. 'I want to talk to you. Come into the drawing room and have a nightcap with me.'

'I don't drink,' she said flatly.

'Of course. Your condition.'

'I am not a condition. The word you are avoiding is *pregnant*,' she said, deliberately running her hand over her gently swollen stomach. 'The reason we're married, remember?' She was tired, fed up, and badly needed to be alone.

'How can I forget?' Conan muttered, and, catching her

arm, urged her into the drawing room. 'But you and I need to talk.'

Shaking off his arm, she walked past him and, kicking off her shoes, sank down into an over-stuffed armchair, curling her feet beneath her, and looking anywhere but at Conan.

A minute later he stood before her, a glass in his hand. 'This won't harm you—it's a St Clement's.'

Josie glanced up and took the glass from his hand; the light brush of his fingers against her own sent a tingle of electricity zinging up her arm. Hastily she took a gulp of the drink. 'What is it?' To her astonishment Conan began to sing a couple of lines of a nursery rhyme completely off key.

'"Oranges and lemons said the bells of St Clement's. I owe you five farthings, said the bells of St Martin's." Surely you know the rhyme?' Conan drawled mockingly. 'And you about to be a mother. The drink is a mixture of orange and lemon—nothing sinister.'

A brief smile flickered across her face and she drained her glass.

'You look like you needed that, Josie. I can't think why. I thought the evening went very well.'

'I'm glad you think so,' she snapped, not at all inclined towards idle conversation. She had had enough of that for one night. 'What did you want to talk about anyway?' she demanded bluntly.

'Do I have to have a reason for talking to my wife?' Conan queried silkily.

Josie's head jerked up at his tone of voice. His dark eyes were narrowed angrily, his mouth tight, and once again she was aware of the man of steel beneath the civilised exterior she had grown accustomed to.

'No, no, of course not, but it has been a very long day and I am rather tired,' she offered. The last thing she needed was to argue with him. She might find herself demanding to know about his relationship with Angela, and it had nothing to do with her. Putting her glass on the side table and uncurling her feet, she prepared to get up. But before her feet touched the ground she was swung up in two strong arms.

'What...?' she exclaimed, and grabbed wildly at his shoulders.

Conan, his anger replaced by amusement, chuckled at the startled expression on her small face. 'In that case, Josie, I will take you safely to bed, hmm?'

'Put me down!' He had removed his jacket earlier, and her hand inadvertently slipped beneath the collar of his shirt. She could feel the heat of his bare skin beneath her fingertips, and she saw the wicked glint in his dark eyes.

'Put...put me down!' she reiterated sharply as he mounted the stairs, but he ignored her plea. She tried to struggle but it was no contest. He was so much bigger and so much more determined.

He strode along the landing and straight into the bedroom, where he dropped her unceremoniously down in the middle of the bed. 'Now, Josie, tell me what's gone wrong. You were all sweetness and light last night and this morning. But this evening you've been like a cat on a hot tin roof. What's changed?' he demanded hardily.

'Nothing.' She swallowed hard and tried to sit up, but Conan stopped her by placing his large hands on her shoulders and pushing her back against the pillows. His long body stretched out on the bed beside her.

'Will you let me up?' She pushed ineffectually at his chest.

'No.'

This morning she had dreamed of Conan in her bed, but now it was a reality she was horrified. She glanced frantically around the room; her eyes alighting on the door to

Conan's room. 'Does Jeffrey know we don't sleep to-gether?' she blurted out then couldn't believe she'd said it.

Conan rolled over her. Leaning on his elbows, he cradled her head in his hands. 'What made you ask that now? You've never been curious before.'

'I just wondered,' she breathed, lifting her hands to his chest in an attempt to push him away.

'Well, don't. Jeffrey does not know. I'm a very tidy man. I make the bed myself before he arrives in the morning. A male ego thing. I do have some pride.'

'Oh.' She blushed; it had been a stupid question, but, worse, the warmth of his body, the weight of his long leg slung over hers, trapping her beneath him, and the attractive face with the beginnings of a five-o'clock shadow only inches from her own, were playing havoc with her over-stretched emotions.

'"Oh"? Is that all you have to say?' he prompted, his long fingers stroking through her hair. 'At my magnificent sacrifice?' he murmured against her ear.

Josie swallowed hard; she had an overwhelming urge to taste the brown satin skin of his throat only inches away from her mouth. Instead she mumbled idiotically, 'Thank you.' Her fingers splayed over his chest in another attempt to push him away.

'Is that the best you can do?' Conan's dark eyes glittered. He knew perfectly well how he affected her and took full advantage of the fact. 'A freely given kiss might be some compensation,' he suggested huskily.

He was deliberately teasing her, she knew, and for a second anger overcame her common sense. 'Only a kiss?' she charged, wondering what Angela had given him, sure that it had not stopped at a kiss. Arching one delicately shaped brow, she added provocatively, 'You're cheap!' Lifting her head, she pressed her lips to his mouth. One kiss and she would be rid of him, was her last clear thought.

Her eyes fluttered closed as she opened her mouth to the pressure of his and their tongues met and stroked. The feel of his hard body sent shock waves of sensual awareness shuddering through her. She forgot about Angela, Charles, everything, as warmth spread from the pit of her stomach to flood her slender body with a delicious sensual lethargy she had never known existed before.

Her hands lingered on his chest, and instead of pushing him away she began exploring intimately under his open shirt, entangling her fingers in his crisp body hair with tactile pleasure. Something so fantastic could not be wrong...

She heard his sigh—or was it a groan?—and opened her eyes. The room was in shadow, the bedside lamp casting a small pool of light around the large bed. Josie stared up at Conan, her huge violet eyes luminous with an expression as old as Eve that she was completely unaware of. Conan was watching her, waiting, his huge body strangely tense.

'You said you were tired, Josie; perhaps I should help you undress?' he offered, and, leaning up on one elbow, he slipped his other hand under the shoulder strap of her dress. 'Tell me, do you want me?' he paused. 'To help you?' he asked throatily.

What on earth was she doing? The question lingered in her mind for all of a second. Then Conan's large hand splayed over her naked shoulder, his long fingers idly caressing her soft skin. She trembled but recognised the unspoken question in the fiery depths of his dark eyes. 'Yes, please,' she murmured, knowing fully well what she was inviting as her fingers, on a voyage of discovery of their own, slid down his chest and tried to unfasten the remaining buttons of his shirt.

'Allow me,' he said huskily. 'I want to look at you.' In one lithe movement he shrugged off his shirt and gently pushed her dress down to her waist, exposing her naked breasts to his gaze.

'You are perfect, absolutely perfect!' Conan groaned, and, lowering his huge body over her, he gently rubbed his broad chest against her achingly sensitive breasts, while his tongue flicked teasingly around the outline of her mouth. Josie's lips parted, begging his kiss, and, unable to resist her offer, his mouth closed over hers in erotic possession.

She felt his welcoming weight move restlessly against her, the heat of his body scorching through her, melting any lingering inhibitions. Her hands curved around his back and traced the indent of his spine, while Conan, with his lips and tongue, encouraged her to take her fill of him. The outside world ceased to exist; they were encapsulated in their secret world of the senses. Josie gave herself up to the pleasure only Conan could arouse in her.

He broke the kiss to trail a line of tiny kisses down her throat to the soft curve of her breasts. Her breasts hardened beneath the gentle flick of his tongue, aching for a more intimate caress. Instead Conan drew back, and she almost cried out in frustration, but he was not to be hurried.

His eyes gleamed golden with desire as he gazed down at the twin creamy globes, the rosy tips dark and rigid. 'For such a small girl you are remarkably well endowed,' he said raggedly, and with one long finger he traced slowly, seductively around the aureole.

A deep shudder streaked from her breast to her thighs, her body arching under him. Her small hand gripped his arm, her fingers digging into his flesh. But with the same slow deliberation he gently caressed her other breast. Josie had never in her life imagined such exquisite pleasure. 'Conan,' she moaned, helpless beneath his sensual expertise.

'I think you like that, Josie.'

'Yes, yes,' she cried, unconscious of how erotically exciting her frantic cry was to Conan.

'And this even more,' he growled, his head dipping and his mouth closing over the rigid tip of her breast.

Josie's breath stopped in her throat as with mouth and tongue he teased first one pert nipple and then the other. Her hands clasped his broad shoulders, urging him closer. Tomorrow she would be ashamed of her behaviour, but now the only thought in her head was Conan. He was a fire in her blood more potent than any drug. She gasped as he shaped her breast with his hands and she drowned in the achingly delicious sensations he ignited in her. She knew it was wrong—he did not love her—but with his dark head at her breast she could not think, only feel. He lifted his head and her eyes sought his with unashamed longing.

'Don't look at me like that, Josie. My control is stretched to the limit as it is,' he said with a low chuckle. 'And I haven't finished helping you undress yet.'

Caught staring, Josie flushed scarlet. 'No need to blush, little one.' Bending over her, he gently eased her dress over her hips and off, and, slipping his fingers beneath the waistband of her briefs, he dispensed with them the same way.

Josie lay quivering on the bed as his large hands traced from her ankles to her thighs. He knelt on the bed beside her, devouring her with his eyes.

'You are so exquisite, Josie!' Sliding his hands up over her breasts, he slipped them under her arms and gathered her up to him. 'And I want you. How I want you.' Then his passionate mouth claimed hers and she shuddered with excitement as together they plunged into the erotic world of the senses.

With teeth and tongue and mouth they breathed the essence of each other, and finally, when they needed to breathe, Conan urged Josie back down on the bed, his hands, his mouth tantalising and tormenting her, learning every throbbing inch of her until every nerve in her body was on fire for him. His eyes dark pools of molten desire, he stared down at her then slowly lowered his head. His mouth found hers, and he kissed her with a fierce, demanding passion that would not be denied. With one hand he traced over the gentle curve of her stomach, his long fingers tangling in the black curls between her thighs, finding the moist, tender flesh that pulsed at his touch.

Josie could not control the whimper that escaped from her parted lips at the ecstasy of his caress. Her nails dug into the hard muscles of his back. The blood surged through her veins, her heart racing till she thought it would explode.

She exulted in their mutual desire, her tongue exploring every contour of his hot, moist mouth. Never in her wildest dreams had she thought it could be like this. But suddenly there was no more time to think as Conan deftly removed his trousers and rolled completely over her, slipping his hard thigh between her slender legs.

She felt the shift in weight of his body, and his aroused hardness as he lifted his head, his jaw rigid as he fought for control. 'You want me, Josie?'

'Yes,' she moaned. She could not help herself; her eyes deepened to purple with passion, staring blindly up at him. She had forgotten the past—everything. There was only now and Conan and an unbearable longing to have him possess her completely.

'Say it, Josie. Tell me.' His almost-black eyes burnt into hers as he rasped, 'I need to hear you say my name. I want you to know it's me and not Charles.'

Josie tensed involuntarily as his whispered words penetrated her sensation-soaked brain, and for a second she remembered Charles and how it had been. Blind, unreasoning panic stormed through her.

'No, no,' she cried, in instinctive rejection, her hands falling from his chest, while her body stiffened in fear.

'No. You said no,' he groaned, shaking his dark head in stunned disbelief.

For a second Josie had frozen, but only for a second. She reached out to Conan, but her hand met only air as, with a string of violent curses, he flung himself off her and lay flat on his back, his massive chest heaving with each rasping breath.

What had she done? Josie asked herself, battling to control her frantically beating heart. She had been terrified for a moment, but only for a moment, and then she hadn't wanted him to stop. She reached out again.

But he swung his long legs to the floor and turned his back on her. 'I've met some women in my time, but you, Josie! What the hell do you think you're playing at? You have a lot to learn if you think you can get away with that kind of teasing.'

'I... I...' What could she say? She should never have let it go so far. She stretched out her hand and gently touched him. She felt his shoulders tense and as he stood up so her hand fell away he spun around to stare down at her.

She tried again. 'I didn't mean...' She began to explain. 'I thought I...' She stumbled to a halt, defeated by the blazing anger leaping like flames in the depths of his eyes.

'I know what you thought. You made that painfully obvious,' he snarled derisively.

She glanced up at him and just as hastily looked away. He was towering over her, unconscious of his naked state. It was more than she could bear.

'You belatedly remembered Charles, didn't you? Didn't you, Josie?' he reiterated scathingly.

'Yes, but...' She had remembered Charles, but not in the way Conan thought! She wanted to explain, but never got the chance.

'I should have known,' he sneered, picking his trousers up off the floor and straightening up. 'What were you doing? Pretending I was Charles, no doubt.' His face hardened. 'Well, let me tell you I have no intention of being a stand-in for a dead man.'

'No, no, it wasn't like that.' She could not bear to let him think that badly of her. If he would just listen for a moment... 'It wasn't quite like that.'

He eyed her lying naked on the bed, his physical strength intimidating her as he looked down his arrogant nose at her, not a trace of anger remaining in his dark eyes, only cold contempt. 'Then maybe you would oblige me by telling me just what you thought you were playing at. You started this fiasco. You've been giving me the green light for the last two days. You can't blame me for taking up the offer.'

Josie's eyes widened in horror. He was right. She hadn't realised she had been so obvious, but to an experienced man like Conan she must have seemed blatant. But she would not admit it. Not for the world.

'Don't look so surprised; you know you did. What's the matter? Suddenly afraid you were going to get more than you bargained for?'

'No,' she denied. 'I...' Her eyes skidded away from his, lingering on the hard muscles of his chest, the flat plane of his stomach, and lower... She gulped and guiltily jerked her gaze back to his, only to be trapped by the knowing gleam in his eyes.

'But perhaps not enough after all. You really are a sensual little girl. What was it? A few months without a man too much for you? Charles gave you a taste for it and you wanted me to relieve your frustration. I can understand that. I've been too long without a woman myself. Was that the problem, Josie?' he queried silkily.

So he had not made love to Angela this afternoon, Josie realised. But it did not make her feel any better. He was in complete control and she was still deathly afraid of her own turbulent emotions. Pulling herself up to a sitting position, she dragged the sheet over her breasts, her hand tangling in the fabric.

'No,' she murmured in denial. Glancing up at him, she saw that his dark eyes fixed on her held no warmth, no passion, only a kind of clinical determination to discover what lay beneath the surface of her mind. Her anger rose at his impersonal inspection. While she had been reduced to an aching mass of frustration, Conan had no such problem; he was once more his cool, enigmatic self.

'Liar,' he said flatly, his eyes sweeping down to the rapid rise and fall of her breasts beneath the sheet, and back to her face.

Why was she even bothering to try and explain to him? she asked herself, scarlet with embarrassment and anger, his sexual arrogance infuriating her even more.

'Believe what you like—frustration, lust; take your pick; I don't care,' she said bluntly. She just wanted him to get dressed and go. Go, before she gave in to the temptation to fling her arms around him and haul him down beside her again.

'No, I don't suppose you do.' Casually he pulled on his trousers and stared down at her, studying the violet eyes that looked too big for the small oval of her face, the love-swollen lips. 'Charles still haunts you, I think.' His cold eyes slid assessingly over her slight form. 'Amazing—' he shook his dark head '—how a beautiful, intelligent woman can be so tricked by a man and the myth of love.'

'Thanks very much.' Josie did not need Conan to tell her that. She had realised it for herself this afternoon. But months too late.

CHAPTER FIVE

CONAN chuckled, a humourless sound, and, fastening the zip of his trousers, he glanced back down at her. 'Surely you don't imagine for a moment that Charles would have remained celibate and grieved over you if the position had been reversed?'

'That's a rotten thing to say,' Josie shot back. Conan would not listen to her, would not let her explain her flash of fear. So let the swine think what he liked. If he thought she still loved Charles all the better. At least Charles had said he loved her. Conan had made no such pretence.

'Rotten but true,' Conan drawled cynically. 'You didn't know him at all, Josie. He didn't care a damn about you. I'd hazard a guess the first time he asked you out was the first time we met, simply because he saw I was interested.'

'No,' Josie denied automatically. But Conan was right; how had he known?

'Charles was always like that, even as a boy. Anything I had or showed the slightest interest in he took or destroyed. The irony of it was, when I was younger I actually looked up to him, but I soon learned. He took my toys, my first girlfriend, and eventually my heritage.'

'No, I don't believe you. Charles wasn't like that.' It couldn't be true, but deep down she had a nasty feeling it was. Remembering the church fête, Charles could have introduced her to his half-brother then. But he'd dismissed him as a virtual stranger.

'Believe what you like. But your knight in shining armour was a louse. He never had the slightest intention of marrying you.'

Josie watched him pull his shirt back on, and had the oddest feeling Conan was enjoying telling her this. Did he want to shame her completely?

'I forced him to get engaged to you, because I thought it was appropriate under the circumstances.'

'No. No, Charles asked me. He said he loved me,' she argued.

'I'm sure he did, but it was a ploy to get you into his bed, nothing more.' His chiselled mouth tightened. 'He always delighted in destroying beautiful things.'

Josie shivered and pulled the sheet up around her chin, an icy dread seeping into her bones as she listened to Conan's cold explanation of her affair with Charles.

'He agreed to marry you only when I insisted on telling Father. You know why? Money.' He answered his own question with blunt cynicism. 'The estate has been badly managed for years, always in the red, and my dear half-brother never lived on his army salary. I bailed the Major and Charles out over and over again. I only had to mention the quarterly accounts that night and Charles fell in line. It was I who got him to agree to marry you,' he said callously. 'Maybe I should have let you find out for yourself what he was truly like. Instead he's enshrined in your memory like some hero—'

'He did die a hero,' Josie cut in defiantly.

One dark brow arched sardonically. 'Sorry, no, Josie; even that was a sham. My father invented the story to save his pride. It was all handled very discreetly. Why do you think there was nothing in the press, no commanding officer and no great military funeral?'

Her brows drew together in a puzzled frown. The funeral in the local church had been small, but it had never occurred to her to question the speed of it or the lack of publicity surrounding the affair.

'Charles was actually killed by a landmine, but not on

duty. He was out with his commanding officer's wife at the time. Charles and the lady had taken a Jeep and driven into the countryside for an illicit night of passion. The deserted road they took had not been cleared of landmines and their passion cost them their lives. She had been his mistress for over a year. You probably met her. A redhead. She was at the party the night Charles got engaged to you. As I said, he liked other people's possessions,' he told her with a cool smile.

Josie closed her eyes. She couldn't bear to look at Conan. She knew instinctively he was telling her the truth. Heavens! She had even met the woman. Charles's mistress! She'd thought at the time they seemed rather close.

Josie had accepted she'd been foolish in her relationship with Charles almost immediately he had gone to Bosnia. Now she cringed in shame at how blind she had been. All the signs had been there for her to see, and she had ignored every one. But at least with Charles she could blame it on drink. With Conan she had no such excuse.

'Nothing to say, Josie? No jumping to Charles's defence?' Conan demanded dryly.

'Yes,' she started to argue, but, looking up at the hard, ruthless planes of his face, she thought better of it. 'No, I think you've said it all,' she managed to answer steadily.

'Very well.' With a dismissive shrug of his broad shoulder he added, 'I'll wish you goodnight.' He walked out.

Josie watched the door close behind him, and shivered. She snuggled back down in the bed, pulling the sheet firmly around her. She was dog-tired, but sleep eluded her. She burned with frustration and anger—at herself as well as Conan. She buried her head in the pillow, but the lingering scent of Conan tormented her senses, and restlessly she rolled on her back to stare with sightless eyes at the ceiling.

In the long, lonely hours before dawn she finally faced up to herself, and she did not like what she saw.

How could she have behaved with such wanton abandon? She did not know. The only thing she was sure of was her shameless desire to have Conan back in her bed, to finish what he had started. If that made her wanton, then she was. And Conan—what of his feelings? He had been right when he had accused her of encouraging him. She had…and she could not blame him for being furious when she had so abruptly stopped him, even though she wished she hadn't.

He was a virile man who by his own admission had been too long without a woman. Obviously because his mistress, Angela, had been in America. Tonight Conan had spent the evening in the company of the woman he loved but for propriety's sake he had had to watch Angela leave with her brother. It was not surprising he had made love to Josie. It must have been frustration at not being able to have his girlfriend; sheer lust.

Josie groaned, disgusted with herself, and finally admitted what her subconscious mind had known all along. She had been attracted to Conan from the first day she met him. The sophisticated stranger with the outrageous comment. But she had never expected to see him again and had quite happily gone out with Charles. How wrong she had been. But it was too late now for regrets.

Josie caught her breath, a slow, grim smile curving her mouth. There was one good thing to come out of this evening. She no longer doubted that what Conan had said about Charles was true, even if he had been trying to hurt her with his revelations.

Conan had inadvertently lifted the weight of guilt she had borne for ages, thinking Charles had loved her, and knowing if he had lived she could never have returned the feeling. The thought of Charles touching her again made her flesh creep. Secretly she had been relieved, after the shock of his death had worn off, that he never would.

She had willingly accepted Conan's offer of marriage, sure she could handle a marriage of convenience for the benefit of her child, conceited enough to think she could live with a man like Conan and feel nothing. But during all these weeks living with him she had got to know the man beneath the expensive suits and, unfortunately for her, fallen in love with him. The last man in the world who could ever love her in return. She had no illusions on that score.

Heavens! He had virtually caught her in bed with his half-brother—the father of her child...

Tonight Conan's reaction had been that of any red-blooded male to a more than willing woman. Love did not enter into it. Conan was a businessman; he had quite simply made a deal with her—the Manor in exchange for giving his name to her unborn child.

No matter what happened in the future, the child she was carrying would always come between Conan and herself, an ever-present reminder. She had to face facts and get on with her life. From this moment on, Josie vowed, she would be strong. She linked her fingers over the soft mound of her stomach, fiercely protective of her unborn child. Her baby was innocent and deserved all her love, and she was going to make sure her child wanted for nothing.

Tomorrow she would go back home; it would be nice to see her father again. She had read somewhere that the first few months of pregnancy were the worst, with massive hormonal changes to the female body. Maybe she could blame her behaviour tonight on that, put the past firmly behind her, and begin to make a life for herself and her child that did not include Conan or any other man.

Conan had been good to her, helping her when she needed it, but now she could return the favour by getting out of his life and giving him a clear field with Angela, even though the thought of them together broke her heart.

Her mind was made up. She would leave tomorrow when Conan was at work, and if the world saw her as a coward for running away, so be it. She knew it was for the best, and finally she fell into a restless sleep.

However, when Josie walked into the kitchen the next morning, a little after ten, she froze, and her plan flew out of the window. Conan was standing by the cooker, unaware of her presence. Why wasn't he at the office? For a long moment she feasted her eyes on him. His broad back was clad in a soft grey sweater, his long legs clearly defined in snug-fitting faded denim jeans. Then he turned.

'Josie. I expected you to sleep in this morning. Jeffrey has the morning off and I was about to bring you breakfast in bed,' he said coolly, then grinned, taking in her rumpled appearance at a glance. The baggy, faded black tracksuit was comfortable but did nothing to enhance her femininity.

'What are you doing here?' she demanded, then nervously tucked a strand of hair behind her ear as the smile left his face to be replaced with a hard-eyed stare.

'I live here, remember?' he prompted sarcastically.

'But you should be at the office.'

He shrugged. 'I'm the boss.' His eyes narrowed on her face. 'You look terrible—trouble sleeping, no doubt. Sit down before you fall down; I'll get you a coffee.'

'Thanks very much,' she snapped, irked that he had known at a glance she had not slept properly all night, whereas he looked disgustingly fit. His black hair, slicked back, still damp from the shower, curled gently on the nape of his neck. It was obvious he'd had no bother sleeping.

'Sarcasm does not become you, Josie. Do as you're told and sit down,' he commanded, and she did. Placing a steaming mug of coffee in front of her, he ordered, 'Drink that and you'll feel better.'

Josie grasped the mug in both hands, raised it to her lips and took a huge swallow, almost scalding her mouth in the process. She shot a wary look at Conan through the cover of her thick lashes. His back was half turned towards her as he deftly arranged scrambled eggs and toast on two plates. Suddenly her stomach turned over at the smell.

He swung around, a plate in each hand, and caught her watching him. She felt the shaming colour flood her face and hastily took another gulp of coffee. A plate of food appeared on the table in front of her. She was aware of him sliding into the seat opposite, but was incapable of lifting her head. It was worse, much worse than she had ever imagined. Last night had made her even more intensely aware of him, if that was possible.

'Eat, Josie; you'll feel a whole lot better. Then we'll talk. I always think there's nothing like a good breakfast for starting the day. Don't you agree?' he asked, and proceeded to tuck into the food on his plate with obvious pleasure.

'Yes, I suppose so,' Josie mumbled in reply and, lifting her fork, made herself eat. Every mouthful tasted like sawdust. His, 'Then we'll talk,' had her nerves stretched to breaking point. She didn't dare look at him, but kept her eyes fixed on the pine boards of the breakfast table.

'You can look at me, Josie. I haven't grown two horns and a tail since yesterday,' he drawled mockingly.

She lifted her head; his golden-brown eyes were very bright. He knew exactly how embarrassed she was.

'I didn't think you had,' she rejoined, sounding much more confident than she felt.

'Good. Last night—'

'Please,' she interrupted. 'Can we forget about last night?' But he was not about to let her off so lightly.

'No, Josie, we can't. You can't bury your head in the sand for ever,' he said quietly. 'However much you may like to.' Pushing the plates to one side, he caught her small hand in his much larger one. His touch sent every sensible thought out of her head. Helplessly she stared at him. She had thought he would be as reluctant as she was to mention last night, but that was obviously not the case.

'Last night happened, Josie, and you can't pretend it didn't. What we have to decide is where we go from here.'

She paled at his words, and, apprehensive about what was to follow, she rushed into speech. 'Last night was a mistake, a rush of blood to the head or something, and it will never, ever happen again, I can assure you.'

'The blood rushed to a quite different part of my anatomy,' Conan drawled with wicked amusement, and she blushed scarlet.

'Never again,' she repeated, at a loss for words.

'How can you be so sure? You're a married woman now. Do you honestly want to live the rest of your life like a nun?'

His long fingers idly laced with hers, distracting her, and she was incapable of answering him. She wasn't feeling the least bit nun-like—in fact quite the reverse.

'I don't believe you do, Josie. I think,' he murmured, his eyes boring into hers, 'you are a very passionate young woman.' Her hand jerked under his and she tried to pull free, but he would not allow it. 'No, Josie, hear me out. Last night I discovered just what a delightfully sensual woman lurks beneath the almost innocent exterior you present to the world, and I wanted you. Still do,' he admitted casually. 'And I think at first you wanted me. Am I right?' he demanded.

'Yes.' There was little point in denying it. She had been so obvious.

'Thank you. I'm glad you're being honest. I didn't like believing you were using me as a stand-in for Charles *all* the time.' His grip on her hand tightened as he continued in a much harder tone, 'I don't know what made you change your mind—a misplaced attack of conscience, perhaps. But I did a lot of thinking last night and decided the only thing wrong between you and me was the timing. It was too soon for you, and I should have realised that.'

Josie could not believe her ears. She looked around the kitchen—anywhere but at her husband. He was sitting discussing sex as though it were a normal breakfast conversation. She had no idea how to cope with this sophisticated, mature male attitude, and it took all her will-power to lift her eyes back to his; but face him she did.

'Conan, I do not wish to discuss last night. I'm a woman, you're a man. It was lust, pure and simple. Over, finished with.' And, wrenching her hand from his, she leant back in her chair.

'"Pure" is not the word that springs to my mind, but at least you're seeing me as a man—a small step forward,' he said cynically.

Josie suddenly had a vivid mental picture of Conan standing by the bed, the ultimate male animal, naked, aroused, and in his prime. Oh! If only he knew just how much she wanted him; but it was impossible, and if she had any doubts on that score they were quickly dispelled by his next words.

'I should have remembered you were pregnant. Damn it, it is only a couple of months since Charles died! I don't know how I could have forgotten that.' He shook his head in a gesture of frustration, and without meeting her eyes he added, 'I should not have said what I did about Charles; after all, the poor devil is dead.'

'It was the truth, though, wasn't it?'

'Yes, but I didn't have to disillusion you quite so soon. I could have chosen a better time to tell you.'

'It's not important; it's academic now anyway,' Josie muttered, and, pushing her chair back, added, 'I think I'll go and change.'

'No, wait,' Conan commanded, and reluctantly she sat back down, feeling incredibly weary all of a sudden.

'What I meant to tell you last night before we got side-tracked was that I spoke to your father last week.'

Josie's brow creased in a worried frown. She spoke to her father every week by telephone, but why should Conan want to talk to him?

'It's nothing to worry about,' Conan reassured her. 'As you know the estate hasn't been run properly for years, but I can't afford to spend much time there, so I've employed an estate manager. He's a family man, and obviously he'll need a house. Your father and I have discussed the manager moving into Low Beeches, and then your father can move into the Manor House with the Major.'

'Give up our home?' Josie cried. 'But...but...' What could she say? Her decision of last night to run back to her father, and quietly withdraw from the Zarcourts' sphere of influence, had been well and truly wiped out.

'Surely you can see, business-wise, it's the ideal solution? That's why I'm taking you down there today—so you can talk it over with your father.'

'I don't think it's a good idea. A man likes to have his own home; my father likes his independence.'

'Rubbish. From what I've seen of your father, he's not in the least independent. He's had you running around after him for years,' Conan declared, a thread of steel in his tone. 'And when I suggested it he jumped at the chance. In fact he's already at the Manor. It was I who insisted he discuss it with you for courtesy's sake, nothing more.'

Josie knew his reading of the situation was right, but it did not make her like it. Her father would be delighted to live with his friend the Major, and with Mrs M., the house-keeper to look after him. But Josie hated the idea. What could she say? Sorry, no. Thanks very much but I'm leaving you and going back to live with my father, and to do that we need to keep our home? If only she dared. She sighed inwardly; it was all such a mess. She glanced at

Conan and his cool, confident smile told her he was not expecting an argument.

'I thought you could spend the next few days sorting out what you want to keep. Then later I'll arrange for the removal of the rest. Your father and mine are each to have their own apartment once the renovations to the Manor House are complete. What do you say?' Conan prompted.

'Yes. I don't know. I suppose so,' she mumbled. But inside she was fuming. 'You seem to have arranged everything to your satisfaction.' But if he noticed the irony in her words he ignored it.

'Good; I'm glad we agree. Now run along and pack. I'll drive you down, but I won't be able to stay, unfortunately. Angela has brought quite a few problems from the New York branch that need my attention. In fact I'll probably have to go over to the USA for a week or so.'

I'll just bet you will, Josie thought bitterly. Did he take her for a complete fool? Conan must have been planning this move for weeks. How convenient that the day after his very feminine American executive arrived, his wife had to go to the country. Still, she could not blame him. He had kept his side of the bargain and married her. She should be grateful, Josie told herself. Anyway, hadn't she decided last night to give Conan a clear field with Angela? Then why did her heart ache to know he had already arranged it for himself?

'Did you hear what I said?' His angry voice broke into her thoughts.

'Sorry, I missed the last part.'

Shoving back his chair, Conan stood up, his dark eyes fixed on her pale face. 'Dreaming about the past again, were we?'

'No.'

'I'm glad to hear it, my de-ear wife.' The drawled endearment made it perfectly obvious he did not believe her.

'For your information I said I should be back by Christmas Eve, if you're interested.' Taking hold of her arm, he pulled her to her feet. 'Now hurry and pack. I have no time to waste.'

Back in her bedroom, a slow-burning resentment at his high-handedness lent force to her actions as she haphazardly stuffed clothes into a suitcase.

Dressed once more in her blue suit—one of the few decent things she had that still fitted her—she cast a last look around the room, and the thought crossed her mind that she would never be here again. She straightened her shoulders, picked up the suitcase, and made her way downstairs and out to the car.

Conan took the suitcase from her hand. 'Is this all? One case?'

Josie waited until he was seated behind the driving wheel before responding, 'Contrary to your mercenary view of women, I don't own a lot and I always travel light.' Unlike his girlfriend with her mink coat and designer clothes, Josie thought spitefully.

Conan turned in his seat and leant over her, ostensibly to fasten her seat belt. But he hesitated, his hand holding the strap resting lightly on her breast. She sank as far back into the soft leather as she could, her breast hardening in quick reaction to his touch.

'An admirable sentiment,' he mocked, his hand pressing slightly against her. Josie knew he was doing it deliberately. But why? 'But not necessary in your case. You have an allowance, credit cards. If it isn't enough just say so. You're my wife; what is mine is yours, and I am a very wealthy man.' After dropping a swift kiss on her soft lips, he deftly clicked the belt into place and was starting the car before she could protest.

She had never touched her allowance; her pride would not let her. Instead she had used her own small savings for the few items she had bought. 'But I'm not really your wife. Ours is a marriage of convenience.' Even as she said it she wished it were not true. But to hope for anything more was to delude herself and she was not going to make that mistake again.

'You're my *real* wife.' Conan shot her a chilling glance, before returning his attention to the road. 'After what almost happened last night I don't know why you bother to deny it. It's only a matter of time.'

'But—' That was as far as she got before he cut her off.

'Drop it. We have a long drive ahead of us. You're tired; put your head back and sleep.'

'I just think…' She meant to say that physical attraction was no basis for a marriage, but never got the chance.

'Your trouble is you think too much,' he derided.

Josie closed her eyes; she had no energy to argue with him, especially when she knew he was right. But she could not stop her mind spinning. Only a matter of time, Conan had said. Did he intend to share her bed in future? Have a real marriage…? No, Angela was his true love… Feeling inexplicably sad, she yawned. She was tired, and trying to understand Conan was giving her a headache.

She imagined she felt the tenderest of kisses on her soft mouth, and she sighed, her eyes fluttering open.

'Wake up, Josie; we've arrived,' Conan was leaning over her, unclipping her seat belt.

She shivered and looked out of the car window. It was snowing and the car had stopped at the foot of the steps leading to the ancient oak entrance door of Beeches Manor. Her own home was gone, and this was all that was left for her. Conan walked around the car and held the passenger door open for her, and something in her expression must have told him how she felt.

'You'll be fine with Mrs M. to look after you, and I'll be back soon,' he said gently.

'I'm sure I will,' she said curtly. Did she really seem so pathetic to him? Stepping out of the car, she added, 'Don't hurry back on my account. I'm perfectly happy to stay with my father; in fact I would prefer it.'

'Maybe so, but you're not going to get the chance.' Conan grabbed her arm and ushered her up the steps and into the house, his expression grim.

Then Mrs M., the housekeeper, was gushing all over them. The grey-haired woman, who was in her sixties, had worked at the Manor all her life, and she gave Josie a hug.

'I'm so pleased to see you and Conan again!' Mrs M. cried. 'And you pregnant and all. Why, this old house has never seen so much excitement in years. Wait until you see my new kitchen—and as for the master suite...'

'Okay, Mrs M.,' Conan cut in. 'You and Josie can gossip to your hearts' content later, but right now I would love a cup of tea and a sandwich.'

'Of course.'

The next few minutes were taken up as the Major and her father greeted the pair of them, and then, with a determined smile, Conan said, 'Excuse us,' and with his arm around Josie's waist he almost carried her up the wide staircase.

'Why on earth did you tell Mrs M. I was pregnant?' she demanded angrily, when they reached the first-floor landing. 'It—'

'Because, my sweet wife, it is becoming rather obvious,' Conan drawled, his long arm reaching right around her waist to splay across her slightly swollen belly. 'And it's about time you stopped trying to play the martyr and started buying some clothes that fit you.'

'Thanks for the compliment; every girl likes to be told she's fat,' she shot back sarcastically.

'Oh, for heaven's sake, Josie, will you stop carping for once, and tell me what you think of the decor?' Exasperation laced his tone as he stopped in the middle of the bedroom.

Silently fuming, she looked around and the first thing she noticed was the elegant ambience, and the second thing she noticed was an enormous bed. There was the door they had entered, and one other on the right-hand side. Slowly she crossed the room and opened the door. It was a magnificent bathroom in Italian marble with a double shower, and a huge circular bath on a raised dais. She closed the door again and turned to Conan.

'Where is your bedroom?' She had a horrible suspicion this was it.

He strolled across to her. One hand came down on her tense shoulders, and she froze. His other hand snaked around her back as he drew her firmly up against him. 'This is my bedroom—yours and mine. Make the most of it for the next few days, because when I return you're sharing it with me.'

'No way!' Josie cried, shoving at his broad chest, and, deliberately taking advantage of her angrily parted lips, he covered her mouth with his own.

Josie stopped breathing, fighting to withhold her response, but he was far too experienced. He chuckled with masculine enjoyment and increased the pressure, his arm wrapping tightly around her, until, with a sigh, she gave in. She trembled violently in his arms as he seduced her with his mouth and tongue, her body on fire for him. Then Conan swung her off her feet, and with a wicked grin he slowly lowered her down his rock-hard body, before freeing her.

He stepped back, his smile triumphant. 'You're not cut out for the celibate life, Josie, however much you try to pretend otherwise,' he observed with ironic amusement. 'That was just a little taste to remember me by. Unfortunately I do have to leave, or I would give you the whole meal.'

'Why, you conceited jerk!' Josie raised her hand, but he caught her wrist when she would have hit him.

'No, simply a husband trying to please his wife,' he mocked. 'Hence the new master suite.' He gestured around the room. 'The rest of the renovations on the house will be completed in about three months.'

'So the Major has signed the estate over to you?' she asked angrily, pulling her wrist free. 'You've got what you wanted!' she almost spat.

'As far as the estate is concerned, yes. A trip to Cheltenham, to sign a few papers, and that was it.' His dark face sardonic, he added, 'As for getting what I want, I'm still working on that, as I think you know, Josie.'

'I am not sleeping with you, Conan,' she blurted out. 'That wasn't part of our bargain.'

'You will,' he asserted arrogantly. 'But for now we'll go downstairs and you'll behave as a loving wife until I leave.'

'It can't be soon enough for me.'

'Liar, Josie—you want me almost as much as I want you.' His dark eyes roamed with explicit sensual knowledge from her tense face to the wild mass of blue-black curls falling to her slender shoulders. 'When I return I will prove it to you.' His gaze shifted to focus on one single curl falling down over her breast. 'And that's a promise,' he averred softly, before turning and walking to the door.

A trembling sigh escaped Josie. She was trapped by circumstance, but, even more frightening, she was trapped by passion. Conan, with his dark Celtic ancestry, added to his experience of life, could read her like a book. He knew she wanted him, however much she denied it.

'Come on, Josie,' he commanded from the door, and she had no choice but to follow him.

She said very little over the tea and sandwiches they

shared with the two old men in the drawing room. The living arrangements had already been decided. Her agreement was a foregone conclusion. Only when Conan got up to leave and demanded that she see him to the door did she stir herself.

'As you're driving past the Low Beeches, you can drop me off there,' she told Conan, walking out to the car. She might as well check it out now, and she could do with the walk back to clear her head.

'Yes, okay,' Conan agreed, and ten minutes later he stopped the car outside her former home.

'Do you want me to come in with you, Josie? I can wait and drive you back to the Manor—I'm not in that much of a rush.'

She looked out of the car window at the mellow stone building. Her home. Ten years of her life gone, and all because of the man beside her. Schooling her face into a careful blankness, she turned and said, 'No, Conan. I would prefer to do this alone, and I know Angela won't appreciate you being late.'

His dark eyes narrowed and for a fleeting instant she thought he was going to object. 'You're right.' He leaned towards her and she thought he was going to kiss her, but he simply opened the passenger door. 'I'll see you soon.' Before she could slide out of the car, he folded his arms around her waist and leaned forward to rub his cheek against hers in the gentlest caress. 'Go, but be careful.'

Josie watched the car disappear down the road, a sadness in her heart that only intensified as she took the doorkey out of her purse and entered the house. Somehow she already felt a stranger. Going into her bedroom, she glanced around. There was nothing here she needed to keep, she thought sadly. Her doll, the posters on the wall all seemed to belong to a girl who no longer existed. She packed a holdall with a few small items, including a picture of her mother and that was it.

Entering the hall of the Manor House, she shivered, not so much with cold, but with a dread of what the future would bring. This was now her home... Her father, the one person who might have helped her, was perfectly content with the new living arrangements. If she wanted a different future it was up to her to make it for herself. The prospect was daunting, but not impossible, she reminded herself firmly. She could get an apartment of her own; make a life for herself.

The following morning she did just that. A trip into Cheltenham to call at the office of Brownlow's proved very beneficial. No one had been hired to replace her yet. Apparently a succession of temps had been used, and after a conversation with her boss, Mr Brownlow, she made arrangements to go back to her old job on a temporary basis, but to Josie it was the first step to regaining her independence.

Fuelled with success, she also visited her local G.P. It was amazing how the name Mrs Zarcourt smoothed the interview, and she was enrolled in a course of antenatal classes in Cheltenham. Her baby was her first priority, and tenderly she placed a hand on her stomach. Her baby; the thought filled her with delight.

As for Conan, in the days that followed she tried her best not to think of him at all. Josie knew his interest in her was fleeting at best. He might have said he wanted to share a bed with her, but once he had slept with Angela again he would quickly forget about a small, plump, pregnant wife, she told herself firmly, and tried to block him from her mind.

Amazingly Josie slipped back into her old lifestyle very easily. Conan phoned most evenings, but she omitted to tell him she was working. In fact she told him very little. Josie found it impossible to speak normally to him. But, driving back from Cheltenham after the office party the day before Christmas Eve, she had a sudden attack of nerves. Conan had informed her he would be arriving at about seven the next night, and, however much she tried to deny it, she had missed him and was looking forward to seeing him.

CHAPTER SIX

THE bright yellow Mercedes coupé stood on the drive, a huge blue bow tied around it, with 'MERRY CHRISTMAS LOVE CONAN' woven into the fabric.

'But it can't be for me!' Josie exclaimed for the third time.

'Look, lady, just sign here.' The salesman waved a delivery note in front of her face. 'It's Christmas Eve and I want to knock off for the day.'

In a state of shock Josie signed the form and took the keys from the man along with the ownership papers. The sweater she had bought for Conan suddenly seemed pitiful in comparison.

The first shock of the day had been the arrival in the post of Conan's present to the Major and her father. Two tickets for a round-the-world cruise, sailing from Southampton in January for four months. The two old men were in the study, plotting the route they were taking.

Josie opened the car door and slid into the driver's seat. It was the most fantastic present; she could hardly believe it. She had spent the last few days convincing herself she would have no trouble resisting Conan's avowed intention to share her bed when he returned home. She only had to think of Angela... But now she was not so sure. Was she really so shallow as to be bought for the price of a Mercedes?

Yes! she thought impulsively. To pot with pride! It was time she accepted the inevitable. For better or worse she loved Conan, and he must care for her or he would never have given her such a wonderful gift. If he still wanted her,

he could have her... How she ached for him. So why not
fight for him? Angela had already had three husbands. Why
should she have Josie's as well? Conan could have married
the woman any time in the past ten years but he hadn't.
Surely that was a good sign? Josie convinced herself, and
with her decision made she spent the rest of the day in
excited anticipation of Conan's return.

At midnight she followed the Major and her father up
the stairs to bed. Obviously Conan was not coming back
yet. Saddened, Josie slid into the huge bed, closed her eyes
and prayed for sleep.

But the ringing of the telephone had her eyes flying open.
She felt for the receiver on the bedside table, and pressed
it to her ear.

'Josie! How are you?' It was Conan's deep, sexy voice
that echoed down the line, making her pulse race. But she
made herself respond casually.

'Fine. Where are you? We all thought you'd be here by
now.' She used the 'we' deliberately, rather than admit she
had been waiting for him all evening.

'I'm still in New York. A snow storm has closed
Kennedy Airport.' She could hear the exasperation in his
tone. 'I am sorry, Josie; I've tried everything, including a
charter, but it's hopeless.'

Relief flooded through her. It wasn't his fault he was
delayed. 'Don't worry, what's a day or two between
friends?' she said with a smile.

'But I really wanted to be back for Christmas, and I'm
afraid it's going to be more than a day or two. Even if it
clears up tomorrow, I have to be back here by Friday. The
problem is more complicated than I thought. I won't bore
you with the details.'

Josie's heart sank. He had only intended spending forty-
eight hours with her anyway, it seemed. Why did she keep
deluding herself he might care?

'Please do tell…' She meant to sound sarcastic but only sounded breathless.

'The bank extended a large loan to a Japanese-American corporation, and it's in a spot of bother—nothing I can't handle. But enough about me. How are you, Josie? Not running around after your father and mine, I hope.'

'Hardly. They got your present, and have been studying maps all day. What made you give them a cruise?' she couldn't help asking.

'Mainly because they're both too old to live in a house with builders and decorators all over the place.'

'That was considerate of you.'

'I'm a considerate kind of guy. Hadn't you noticed?' he asked, with a chuckle that made her heart spin.

Belatedly she remembered the car. 'Yes, I had, and thank you for the car. I love it, but really there was no need. I can drive Dad's.'

'No, you can not. A new car was a necessity; that old rust-bucket of your father's is ready for the scrap heap, and you can't risk your baby's life, let alone your own, in that thing.'

Some of the shine went out of the gift for Josie at his comment. 'Well, thank you again; it's very nice.'

'You can thank me properly when I get back—or improperly if you like,' he drawled sexily.

Her stomach clenched with a shaft of longing so intense, she almost moaned. Instead she wriggled under the bed-clothes and the safety of the distance between them gave her the confidence to respond daringly. 'I might just do that, Conan. But what exactly do you mean by improperly?' She heard his swiftly indrawn breath, and grinned.

'Josie! Now you ask, when the Atlantic is between us! What are you trying to do to me?'

'Encourage you to return. This bed is far too big and

cold for me alone.' She chuckled out loud at her own audacity.

'Why, you little tease!' Conan laughed. 'I hope you're as brave when I'm in bed with you.' His voice dropped. 'Every luscious inch of you naked, exposed for my eyes only. I want to sip at your breast, and taste you with my tongue until you're delirious with desire.' It was his turn to tease and it was Josie's turn to catch her breath at the image he evoked in her mind's eye.

'Yes, well… Do you realise what time it is? One o'clock in the morning,' she said inanely to cover her pounding heart.

'The next time we talk at one in the morning I'll be in bed with you, and I won't let you change the subject so easily—that's a promise,' he declared huskily. 'But I'm sorry for waking you, though I wouldn't have missed this conversation for the world. I'll be back as soon as I can.'

'Make it quick,' she breathed, her body flushed with heat, and then a sudden attack of nerves had her adding, 'Happy Christmas, but if you don't mind…' She paused.

'You're tired; I understand. Give my regards to the old men. And, Josie I really am sorry I can't be with you, but Angela has tried everything without success.'

Josie stiffened, the mention of Angela enough to cool her overheated flesh. 'Tell her thanks, but…' she yawned loudly '…I really must get some sleep.'

'I know, darling. Merry Christmas. I'll be thinking of you, and I'll be back by next Tuesday at the latest.'

'Don't hurry on my account,' she said, more sharply than she had intended, but the mention of Angela had been enough to dent her optimism.

'I'll see you soon,' were the last words she heard as she replaced the receiver.

Josie curled up in bed, and replayed the conversation in her mind. She loved Conan, totally, and the sound of his

voice alone was enough to make her ache with frustrated
desire. But it was going to be almost another week before
she saw him. In the meantime he was with Angela! Though
that did not necessarily mean he was sleeping with the
woman, she told herself staunchly. Whatever the reason for
their marriage, Josie knew when Conan held her he wanted
her. Even a man of his experience couldn't fake his body's
reaction so convincingly. She had decided it was time to
give Conan the benefit of the doubt, and their marriage a
chance, and she was not going to change her mind now.
When he returned she would be a loving, sexy wife and
maybe propinquity would do the rest.

By the following Monday, when she drove her new car
into Cheltenham to work, she was almost happy. But when
the telephone rang at nine the next night the burgeoning
hope she had entertained of starting a meaningful relationship with her husband was killed stone-dead...

It was Angela, calling from London. Conan had asked
her to relay a message. He was still delayed in America,
but he hoped to be back by the weekend. Josie might have
believed the message was genuine, had it not been for the
background noise of a party in progress, and a whispered
aside she was not supposed to hear.

'Shhh, Con; she might hear you and guess you're already
back,' Angela drawled huskily.

Josie carefully replaced the receiver, and, using tiredness
as an excuse, she said goodnight to the old men and walked
upstairs.

Stripping off her clothes, she asked herself, Why? Why
did she torture herself so? She had known from the start
her love was hopeless. Josie stared at the engagement ring
and gold band on her finger. They were only for appearance's sake, as was her marriage. She had to stop fooling
herself. She had to block Conan out of her mind once and
for all.

Josie tried. She drove the Major and her father down to Southampton for their cruise, and waved a cheery goodbye. The weekend came and went with another brief telephone call from Angela. Conan was still delayed. With a heightened sense of determination Josie spent her time reading the book on childbirth she had bought, and started massaging her swollen stomach with baby oil religiously every night. The baby was her only priority.

Walking into the kitchen on Wednesday morning, Josie sighed at the grim expression on Mrs M.'s face. The old lady did not approve of her working, and Josie listened in silence as the housekeeper declared that it had snowed all night, and Josie had to be mad to go out.

Ignoring the dire warning, and driving in to the office, Josie told herself she felt better than she had done in months. A new year, a new life, new hope. Who needed a man?

But at five-thirty in the evening, when she parked her car and walked into the dimly lit hall of the Manor, her confidence took a nose-dive.

'So you're finally home!'

She jumped in surprise, the familiar deep, sexy voice shaking her to the core. Conan was leaning nonchalantly against the wood frame of the sitting-room door. Over six feet of solid muscle that the conservative business suit he wore could not tame. Every nerve in her body tightened in direct response to the sensual impact of the man. Nothing had changed. Josie swallowed a groan, frozen to the spot, intensely aware of him.

'What are you doing here? I didn't see your car,' she said, her voice higher than she would have wished.

'I parked it round the side,' Conan straightened and moved towards her, his dark golden eyes glinting with mocking amusement. 'I thought to surprise my wife, but then I was expecting a more enthusiastic greeting from you,' he drawled, and, pulling her unresisting figure against the hard length of his, he covered her mouth with his own.

Only when she was breathless and trembling in every limb did he break the kiss. Looking down at her and noting her dazed violet eyes he said smoothly, 'That's more like it. Happy Christmas, Josie.'

Drawing a deep breath, she battled against her wayward senses, and, schooling her features into what she hoped was a polite smile she responded, 'Happy Christmas, Conan.' Pushing her hands against his broad chest, she added, 'But you're a bit late. It was two weeks ago.' Her legs were like jelly, his kiss had shaken her to her bones, but she did not want him to see it, and, brushing past him, she made straight for the sitting room, disturbingly aware of him following her only a step behind.

Sinking on to the nearest sofa, Josie glanced up at him towering over her. He looked rakishly handsome, his tie loose and his shirt unfastened at the neck, but the gold glint in the dark eyes that captured hers hinted at danger.

'Not quite the eager response I was hoping for,' he drawled sardonically.

'Sorry… But in my experience one rarely gets what one hopes for.' Josie's voice was tight. Ten days ago she had thought their marriage might have a chance, but no more… Deliberately she fixed her gaze on his chest, and asked the question that had been burning in her brain for a week.

'When did you get back from America?' Would he admit that he had been back in England since last week? she wondered. But not by a blink of an eye did she betray her thoughts. Instead she tagged on, 'Did you solve the problem?'

'I flew in this morning and, yes, I managed to sort everything out successfully.' She could feel the intensity of his gaze on the top of her head, and she knew he was puzzled by her less than enthusiastic welcome 'You're angry because I didn't get back for the holiday, but I did ring.'

'Yes, Angela gave me your message,' she said coolly. He had some nerve reminding her...

'I didn't mean just Angela. I rang and spoke to the Major because you were out. He did tell you?'

'No, he must have forgotten.' What a liar he was. Somehow Josie had always considered Conan to be strictly honest, but now she realised the opposite was true. She lifted her head, her stormy eyes clashing with his. It was amazing how he managed to look sincere. Yet she knew he had spent the last week in London with Angela. Obviously he took her for a complete fool.

'Much the same as you conveniently forgot to inform me you had gone back to work, I suppose,' he prompted with silken softness, his eyes narrowing to slits on her upturned face. It was only then she realised he was savagely furious.

'Yes, well, you weren't here to tell, and Mr Brownlow needed a temporary secretary,' she flung back, refusing to be intimidated by his sarcasm.

'Yes, nothing! What the hell do you think you are playing at?' Not waiting for an answer he ploughed on ruthlessly. 'You're a pregnant woman, for heaven's sake, and my wife. Yet I can't trust you for a moment to look after yourself.'

Josie did not trust Conan full stop! And his listing her as pregnant first and his wife second only served to stiffen her resolve and gave her the strength to put the plan she had been forming in her head into action.

'Ours is a marriage of convenience, as you well know. And it's as convenient for me to work as it is for you,' she said facetiously, and, leaping to her feet, she tried to slip past him.

'Don't be ridiculous! It's not the same at all.' He caught her arm and spun her around to face him. 'Have you no sense—driving around country roads in the middle of winter in your condition? As of now you are going to do as you are told. You will call Mr Brownlow in the morning and tell him you're no longer available, and tomorrow you're returning to London with me.'

Jerking her arm free, she headed for the door, too incensed to speak. So she was ridiculous! Incapable! Now she knew what he really thought of her.

A long arm snaked around her waist and hauled her back against his body. 'Don't you dare walk away from me, Josie. I haven't finished with you yet,' Conan snarled. His hand dug into her side as he swung her around in his arms yet again. Josie felt the frisson of excitement that his touch never failed to arouse and bitterly resented it.

'Well, I've finished with you!' she cried, grasping his arm and trying to wriggle free from his hold. Flinging back her head, she defied him. 'And I am not giving up my job, or going to London with you, or anywhere else.' She was furious. How dared he tell her what to do? She was her own woman, even if she hadn't been behaving as such for a while.

Stark fury flashed in his dark eyes, and the realisation that he was going to kiss her again came too late for Josie to take evasive action. She felt the hard, demanding pressure of his mouth against her own, and tried to keep her lips closed. But the intense passion, the desire in the savagely hungry kiss, made her mouth open to welcome his thrusting invasion. She knew the danger but was helpless to resist, softening against him as he drew all her strength from her with the power of his sexuality. Shame burned through her, but with it a fierce longing she was helpless to control. And when Conan finally raised his head, his breathing ragged, and they stared at each other, it was Conan who recovered first.

'What happened to the soft, sexy woman I spoke to on

Christmas morning, Josie? I don't understand. I can see the desire in your eyes, for heaven's sake! Why deny it?' he challenged in a deep, rasping voice.

Humiliated by her abject surrender to his kiss, she fought to keep her breathing steady and bravely forced her eyes back to his.

'Put it down to my condition and hormones, if you like. But don't try and tell me what to do. You are not my keeper.'

'Oh, but technically I am,' Conan drawled, with a sardonic tilt of one brow.

Colouring furiously, Josie could not deny he had kept her very comfortably for months, and it made her madder than hell! 'Not any more,' she raged. 'I can earn my own living; I don't need some pompous oaf telling me what to do.'

'Why, you...' Conan snarled, his dark glance raking over her with savage intensity. 'You selfish little bitch.' His arm tightened around her, and she raised her hand to ward him off, fearful of this wild-eyed man. Perhaps 'oaf' had been a bit strong, but Conan drove her to it.

'Josie.' He said her name, sensing her fear. Dropping one hand from her waist, he ran it distractedly through his hair. His dark eyes sought hers, a hint of regret in their depths. 'Please, Josie, don't be afraid of me. I'm sorry; I'm not used to dealing with a pregnant woman.'

'You don't have to *deal* with me,' she sneered, but inside she was shaking. She wished he would simply let her go. Talking was getting them nowhere, but the way he was holding her, his hard body pressing lightly against her, was arousing a host of erotic sensations she could not control. She felt her breasts swell against the soft wool of her shirt, and the fact that she was responding to him despite herself only infuriated her further.

'But I want to. I remember how you were in my arms

the last night we were together in London,' Conan reminded her softly.

'Well, I don't.'

'You have a short memory,' he derided, and, lifting his free hand to cup her chin, he added, 'Let me remind you.' With a slight tilt to his mouth, he smiled, and it took all her will-power to resist the deliberate sensual invitation in his gold-flecked eyes.

Josie took a deep, steadying breath, forcing herself to meet his gaze as she put her plan into words. 'No, thanks. I meant what I said, Conan. I am not coming back to London. I'm staying here, and I'll be moving out of this house as soon as I can get an apartment. My work is here, my friends are here, and the area holds special memories for me.'

She nearly choked on the lie she was about to tell. 'I'm sure Charles would have expected me to stand on my own two feet and look after his child.' She watched the smile disappear from Conan's face, but still she carried on. 'I'm going to attend the clinic in Cheltenham until the birth of my baby. It's all arranged. I'm sure you understand; after all, you have friends in London—you don't need me,' she finished smoothly, but inside she was quaking. His arm around her waist tightened, his face flushed dark red.

'When the hell have you ever considered my needs?' he snarled, his fingers gripping on to the side of her jaw. He looked as if he wanted to shake her, but instead he suddenly set her free, and marched across the room to stand looking out of the window with his back to her.

Josie collapsed back on the sofa. His rage had surprised her. She thought he would have been relieved she was giving him a clear field in London with Angela. She glanced at him, and could see the effort he was making to control his temper. His hands were curled into fists at his sides, and she could sense the tension in the set of his wide shoulders.

'You realise the builders are moving in to renovate the rest of the house, and I won't be able to get down here much in the next few months?' Conan finally broke the fraught silence, with a complete change of subject. Then, slowly turning he crossed to where she sat. 'You will be alone with Mrs M. Is that what you want?' he demanded harshly.

'Yes,' she confirmed bluntly.

'You know you would be much better looked after in London. The private clinic is far superior to the cottage hospital here.' Suddenly he bent over her, one hand on the arm of the sofa, the other behind her head on the back of the sofa.

The breath caught in her lungs; he was heart-breakingly close, and she was not sure she could hold out against his lethal charm. 'So you say,' Josie murmured. She could see the fine lines at the corners of his eyes, and she could almost believe it was a pleading gleam in his dark gaze, instead of anger.

'Forget about me, Josie, and think what's best for your unborn child.'

'I have and I'm staying in the country.'

'Is that your final word?'

'Yes,' she said emphatically.

'Right, then,' Conan abruptly straightened up. 'If that's what you want, far be it from me to deny you.' Glancing down at her, he fixed her with a look of such contempt that she cringed. 'I honestly thought it was simply the timing that was wrong between you and me. But I was wrong. You're the worst kind of tease. Promising the world over the telephone. "This bed is far too big and cold for me alone."' He mimicked her own words viciously.

'You know, Josie—' his dark eyes raked her from head

to toe, stripping her with a glance '——I felt sorry for you, caught up with Charles, but I was wrong. No wonder Charles kept a mistress with you as his partner. You have the body of a woman and the mind of a child. In fact I have finally realised you and Charles were the perfect couple—both spoilt children, you deserved each other.'

'It's a pity you didn't come to that conclusion before you married me,' Josie shot back, furious at being called a child; as for the rest, she didn't care.

Conan's lips curved in a knowing smile that never reached his eyes. 'Perhaps you're right. I hope for your sake the memory of Charles will keep you warm in bed at night, but I doubt it.'

'You're never likely to find out,' she snapped back. The thought of Angela warming Conan's bed was never far from her mind, and Josie was tempted to confront him with her suspicions. But her pride had taken such a battering over the last few months, she was determined to hang on to the little she had left.

'No.' One dark brow arched sardonically. 'Of course not. After all, I'm only your husband.' And, leaning back over her, he curved a large hand around her throat.

For a second Josie thought he was going to choke her; then, insolently, he ran his hand down to her breast. She blushed scarlet, but could not stop the tremor that coursed through her as his hand cupped her breast over the fine wool of her shirt, his thumb grazing over the taut nipple ever so lightly, then withdrawing.

'When you're tired of playing games, Josie, give me a ring,' he drawled derisively, fully aware of how his touch had affected her. 'My darling wife,' he ended with icy sarcasm.

She had done it. She had known there had been no love lost between the half-brothers, and that her mention of Charles would make Conan angry. She had not realised quite how angry. She heard him tell Mrs M. he was leaving, followed by the slam of the heavy front door, just before a car engine roared into life. Presumably Conan was going straight back to London, and Angela...

CHAPTER SEVEN

JOSIE drove the yellow convertible tentatively out of the clinic car park. It was over two weeks since Conan had left. It had snowed solidly ever since, causing chaos all over the country, with dozens of roads blocked. Luckily the road from Beeches to Cheltenham had been kept relatively clear, which meant Josie had managed to get to work all right although the journey took a little longer. But today she had not been to work.

Driving slowly out of Cheltenham, Josie glanced at the photograph lying on the passenger seat, a secret smile playing around her lips. She had been to the clinic for an ultrasound scan, and the baby was fine. The grainy picture of the tiny infant was magical.

She turned her attention back to the road ahead; the light was fading, and a severe frost was forecast. Suddenly she felt a brief flicker in her stomach, and she gasped; taking one hand from the steering wheel, she placed it over her stomach. There it was again. Her baby was moving inside her; the thrill was indescribable, and she laughed out loud, her gaze straying once more to the photograph.

It took a second for her brain to register the fact that the car was sliding. A silent scream escaped her. The grinding crash of metal was the last sound she heard, before the darkness swallowed her up.

It was the voices she heard first, coming at her through the darkness.

'The baby is fine, Mr Zarcourt, and your wife, as far as

we can ascertain, has no really serious injury, apart from the blow to her head.'

'But it's been days and she's still unconscious!' a deep voice said angrily. 'You're the expert. Do something.'

It must be her they were talking about. She heard the anguish in the tone, and she wanted to reassure whoever it was. She was fine—and a baby—she was having a baby… She lay motionless, the dull ache in her head gradually easing slightly. Slowly, very slowly, she tried to open her eyes. Everything was misty grey; she moved her head, and winced. Suddenly a dark shape loomed over her. The mist evaporating, her eyes gradually focused clearly.

'Thank God you're all right!' Warm lips brushed her brow, and fiercely glittering eyes stared into hers.

He was big and dark, unshaven and dishevelled. Who was he? Where was she? She looked down, unable to stand the intensity of his gaze. Railings at the bottom of the bed, a square clipboard attached. A hospital. Panicking, her eyes flew back to the man leaning over her. He did not look like a doctor.

'Where am I?' Was that thin sound her voice? Her throat felt sore, her lips dry and cracked as she nervously ran her tongue across them. What was the matter with her? And who was this man sitting on the bed?

Another voice answered. 'Well, Josie, you're with us at last.'

She moved her eyes. Another man stood at the other side of the bed. Older, with white hair, a white coat; a doctor. He smiled down at her.

'Good, so you've finally awakened. You had us all worried for a while, but now a few simple tests and it won't be long before your husband can take you home.'

'Husband?' Her puzzled gaze shot back to the younger man. She lifted her hand to her aching head but the glitter of gold and diamonds arrested her hand in mid-air. 'I'm married?'

'Very much so, my dear; married and pregnant, and I'm happy to say the baby is fine.' The doctor chuckled. 'As for your husband, he has never left the hospital since you arrived—the staff have christened him the Ghost of St Martin's.'

'Oh, St Martin's.' That rang a bell—a nursery rhyme—and her cracked lips parted in a brief smile at the pun.

'You know where you are, Josie?' the deep-voiced man, her 'husband' asked urgently.

She lifted puzzled eyes to the dark-haired man. 'No, a nursery rhyme.' What was the matter with her? She could not remember anything. He had called her Josie, so that must be her name. But what was his name? She had no idea, and she was having his baby... Warily, she studied him. He had a strong, attractive face, and she felt a tiny glimmer of recognition as she gazed into his eyes.

He heaved a deep, heartfelt sigh as she watched, then his lips curled back over gleaming white teeth in a broad smile, and he caught her hand in his much larger one. His clasp was firm, as though afraid she would vanish.

'Don't be afraid, Josie; you and the baby are going to be all right.'

'But what happened? I don't remember, I don't remember,' she repeated, her eyes filling with tears.

'Hush, Josie; please don't cry. You're safe; you are in St Martin's Hospital in London. You were in a car accident, and suffered a nasty blow to the head. It isn't a particularly severe injury, but you have been unconscious for a while. It's natural for you to feel a little disorientated.' The man lifted her hand to his lips and kissed it, and, looking across the bed, he added 'Isn't that so, Dr Ferguson?'

'Yes, yes, of course,' the doctor quickly confirmed. 'But

if you wouldn't mind leaving now, Mr Zarcourt, I can examine your wife thoroughly and put her mind at rest.'

'All right, but I'll be back soon.' He rose to his feet and planted a swift kiss on her dry lips before leaving.

A nurse arrived, and gave Josie a drink of juice, then stood by the bed as the doctor examined her. The doctor continued talking as he took her pulse, shone a light in her eyes, her ears, listened to the baby's heartbeat, subjecting her to a thorough examination. It was only when he asked her how old she was that she realised she still could not answer him. No matter how hard she tried, she could not remember anything.

'My name is Josie. I'm Josie,' she said helplessly.

'Yes, it's alright, Josie.' His kindly voice soothed her. 'You're Mrs Josie Zarcourt, and it's as I thought. You have the classic symptoms of post-traumatic amnesia. The fact you remember nothing from before the accident is not abnormal.'

Amnesia. The word echoed in her head. She was swamped by the most incredible feeling of loneliness, doubting her very existence. 'Please tell me.' She lifted her hand in a pleading gesture. 'Will…will I get my memory back?'

'Don't worry, Josie; that's the worst thing you can do. All you need is rest. You may suffer from headaches, perhaps a little giddiness, but that will pass. Trust me. I'm sure you'll recover your memory completely, but don't try to force it.'

'And the baby?' She ran her hand over the soft swell of her stomach. Unless she was fat, there was no doubt she was expecting a child. 'Oh…' she gasped. 'I felt something move.'

Dr Ferguson chuckled. 'Perfectly natural. You're about five months pregnant, the baby is fine, and so will you be. Tomorrow we'll give you an ultrasound just to make sure everything is as it should be, and in a few days you can go home with your husband. In the meantime the nurse will fill you in on anything else you want to know.'

The nurse gave her a quick wash, and helped her into a clean nightdress, chattering all the time. Her name was Ann, she was unmarried, and she was obviously smitten by Josie's husband.

Josie lay for a long time after she had left, her mind a mass of disjointed thoughts. Dr Ferguson had said 'Don't worry'. She groaned; it was impossible not to. Deliberately she began to list in her head what she did remember. She knew the months of the year, the days of the week. God, religion, the changing seasons.

Then she realised the futility of the exercise. It was not knowledge she had lost so much, but memory. Who was she? Her family? Friends? The hospital was in London, so obviously she lived here. She was married to a man she did not know, and was carrying his child, and yet she did not remember the conception...

Ann, the nurse, walked in. 'Tea and time for your medicine Mrs Zarcourt.'

Josie took the cup of tea, and drank it down thirstily. Then, out of the blue, she was struck by a fierce wave of protective emotion for her child. 'The medication won't harm my baby?' she asked quickly. She could put up with a headache but nothing must harm her child.

'No. Packed with vitamins with a mild sedative effect, it will do both of you the world of good.'

'Josie.' The deep male voice woke her from a light sleep. Cautiously she opened her eyes, and levered herself up into a sitting position, folding the bedclothes over her stomach.

'Ah, Josie. You're finally with us again. You can't imagine how good that makes me feel,' the man said softly, and in a few lithe strides he crossed the room and seated himself on the side of the bed.

Josie's eyes widened in surprise. The dishevelled stranger of when she'd first woken up had been replaced by a tall broad-shouldered, clean-shaven, attractive man, immaculately dressed in a grey suit and white shirt. Warily she studied him. 'Who are you?' she asked inanely, a jumble of emotions churning inside her. If he was her husband she did not even remember his name...

'Conan. My name is Conan. The doctor told me you'd lost your memory but...' He hesitated, a flicker of some emotion she did not recognise illuminating his hard features. 'You really don't remember anything?' he demanded, watching her with dark, assessing eyes.

'No. No. I'm sorry...Conan.' She tried his name. 'Conan,' she repeated softly, the word sliding easily from her tongue. 'Are we really married?' she asked, searching his face, hoping to find some memory, anything that would help her from the fog she was living in. As she watched, his dark glance slid from her face and down over her shoulders to linger for a long moment on her full breasts and the soft swell of her stomach. She had the oddest notion he was undecided as to how to respond.

Then suddenly his head lifted and his glittering eyes clashed with hers. 'Absolutely, Josie,' he declared, and, catching her small hands in his, he squeezed them gently. 'I am your husband, all legal and above board, I can assure you.'

She trembled slightly, suddenly aware of the warmth of his hands enfolding hers and resting on her stomach. 'And we're having a baby,' she murmured.

'That, too,' he confirmed as he slowly bent his dark head towards her, and she could do nothing but stare, mesmerised, as his mouth gently closed over hers. The touch of his lips, the scent of him were somehow familiar. A tingle of excitement fluttered down her spine. Her husband, she told herself. She felt something for this big dark man; the reaction of her body told her as much. His tongue slid between her parted lips and he kissed her with an achingly tender passion.

'Convinced?' He broke the kiss and let go of her hands and pulled her into his arms.

Josie tentatively rested her hands on his chest, and studied his tanned, rugged features. His kiss had aroused a host of emotions inside her. Her response had been involuntary, but still there was a lingering fear she could not dispel. She wanted so much to believe she remembered him, but deep down she was forced to admit that, apart from the brief flicker of recognition she'd felt as she'd first looked into his eyes, he was still a stranger. A handsome one, but a stranger. A shiver of apprehension slithered down her spine as she gazed up at him. There was a hardness about him, a look that almost dared her to deny him... No, she was imagining things. He was here for her, wasn't he...?

'I think so,' she finally answered him. She might be injured, but she would have had to be brain-dead not to realise he was a devastatingly attractive man. Her senses were captivated by his touch, the musky male scent of him, and the warmth of his powerful body was the stuff of fantasy. On impulse Josie added mischievously, 'But you could try again just to make sure!'

It was his turn to look surprised; his dark eyes flared briefly, and his arms tightened around her. She could feel the heavy beating of his heart against her own, then once again his mouth sought hers. The kiss seemed to go on for ever and lit an answering response in Josie. She wrapped her slender arms around his neck. Yes, yes this was real. Josie groaned, and when he ended it she was trembling.

'Josie,' he breathed unsteadily. 'We'd better stop.' Holding her close, with one hand he gently stroked the back of her head as she buried her face in his broad chest.

It was so good to feel the solid warmth of his body, and for long moments she was content to wallow in the protection and comfort he offered her. The sense of loneliness, desolation she had felt after talking to the doctor miraculously disappeared to be replaced with a growing sense of security in Conan's arms. 'I am convinced,' she murmured. 'But I still have no memory.'

'Trust me, Josie.' He gently nuzzled her hair. 'The doctor has explained everything to me, and it will all come back eventually.' Easing her gently back against the pillows, he held her hands loosely in his. 'But in the meantime you must not try to force your memory. I'll answer any questions that are really bothering you. Okay?' He smiled.

'Okay.' She grinned back at him. 'But I have a million questions; I hardly know where to start. First—how did the accident happen? Was I driving? Who else—?'

'Wait. Wait,' he cut in. 'Perhaps it would be better if you listen and I'll tell you what the doctor thinks you need to know.' And he proceeded to do so. 'The accident was unavoidable, and there was no one else involved. You were driving back from the antenatal clinic. There was ice on the road and the car skidded into the ditch. But I blame myself because I allowed you to drive yourself.'

'No, you mustn't blame yourself; it was obviously simply an act of God…or my bad driving.'

'You're very generous, Josie,' his hands tightened around hers. 'But it was my fault. I should never have let you go alone, and I'll never let you go alone again,' he declared fiercely.

'And am I alone? I mean, do I have any family apart from you?' She had to ask because it had occurred to Josie that there had been no mention of any visitors other than Conan.

'Ah, Josie, you cut me to the quick!' He sighed dramatically, placing a hand over his heart, but his dark eyes sparkled with amusement. 'I thought I was enough for you,' he said teasingly, before going on to explain that she had a father, who was currently on a world cruise. He had contacted the ship—it was somewhere in the Indian Ocean, and her father had intended leaving at the next port of call to come back to see her. 'I hope you don't mind, but I called the ship again this afternoon and told him there was no need for him to cancel his cruise—you were recovering fine.'

'Cruising on his own? That sounds lonely,' she murmured.

'Not alone. My father is with him.'

'So our families are friends? That's nice.' She grinned. The information reassured her. Conan was definitely her husband and they were happily married. 'But what about brothers or sisters? Do I have any?'

'No, and your mother died when you were young.'

'Oh. So do you have any siblings I should know?'

He glanced down at their entwined hands. 'No; like you I only have a father.'

She looked at his down-bent head, and frowned. She had the strangest feeling that there was something he wasn't telling her...

Catching her frown, he gave her a reassuring smile and talked on, filling in all the details she needed to know in a calm, reassuring manner: how old she was, where they lived, and his career as a banker.

She looked around the room. It was obviously a private room, tastefully furnished, with pictures on the walls, and an *en-suite* bathroom. 'Is this a private suite, a private hospital?' she asked curiously.

'Yes.' He smiled. 'You have a very wealthy husband, you lucky girl.'

'And a very conceited one,' Josie offered as the nurse bustled through the door.

'Sorry, Mr Zarcourt, visiting is over for this evening, but I must say, Josie, you look much better. I knew your husband would soon put a smile back on your face.'

It was only when Ann mentioned her face that Josie realised she had no idea what she actually looked like...

'You're beautiful,' Conan said softly, and, briefly pressing his lips to hers, he stood up.

He had read her mind. 'How did you...?'

'Because you're mine. My wife.' And the dark golden eyes resting on her gleamed with proud possession.

Much later, as Josie drifted gently into sleep, she smiled softly reliving Conan's parting kiss. Her husband...

In the morning, Josie swung her legs over the side of the bed, a strong arm at her elbow supporting her, but for an instant she felt dizzy.

'Come on, Josie; if you want your hair washed, you have to make it to the bathroom,' Ann commanded.

'It's okay for you,' Josie smiled up at the nurse. 'You haven't been out cold for days.'

She had awakened feeling physically almost normal, but mentally she was still trying to remember her past. But when Ann had walked in with a huge bunch of red roses, the accompanying card reading, 'Love, Conan,' every nagging worry had been pushed from her mind.

Ann washed Josie's hair then left her with some privacy, insisting only that the door must remain open so Josie could call if she needed her.

Standing in front of the mirror over the washbasin, her legs felt a little as if they did not belong to her, and the mirror image of her face appeared equally strange. Large, thick-lashed violet eyes stared back at her with an expression of wary interest. Thick black hair hung in deep ringlets to her shoulders, framing the small oval of her pale face.

Apart from a whopping black and blue bruise from her forehead to her temple, she was pretty, she supposed, though a lot younger-looking than she had imagined. And a lot shorter... A rueful smile curved her full lips.

She glanced down at her naked body, glowing pink from the shower; there was no disguising the round swell of her stomach where her baby nestled. She was getting big. Still, Conan must approve of her looks or he would not have married her, and it was his child that was adding the inches to her waistline.

She sighed, her heart sinking a little. The trouble was, she still did not recognise herself. The thought made her uneasy, and turning, she picked up the nightdress from the negligée set draped over the rail that Ann had left for her, and slipped it over her head. It was exquisite—white silk, with a softly scooped neckline, falling to the floor in gentle folds. She smoothed the fabric over her hips, loving the feel of the fresh-scented material. Conan must have given it to her. Josie stopped in the process of picking up the matching robe. How did she know that? Had she remembered? she wondered, and, slowly slipping the robe on, she frowned. Conan appeared to be a very attractive, sophisticated, wealthy man. Somehow her own image didn't seem to quite match his. But Conan must love her or why would they be married? She hesitated, her hands on the belt of the robe as the thought exploded in her mind. She wanted him to love her... She had no memory of him apart from yesterday, but she instinctively knew she loved him...

CHAPTER EIGHT

HOWEVER, Josie had no time to dwell on her husband, amnesia, or anything else, as the morning was taken up with a scan, and another examination by Dr Ferguson and a female doctor called Dr Masters, who was apparently Josie's obstetrician.

Josie had just finished a late lunch when Dr Ferguson breezed into her room, his kindly face crinkled into a broad grin.

'Excellent news, Josie—your scan was fine. The slight swelling in your brain has subsided, so apart from the bump on your head you're okay.'

She smiled back. 'Does that mean I can leave now?'

'Patience, Josie. In three or four days maybe. Can't wait to get back home with your husband, hmm?'

But Josie was not so sure. 'Well, yes. No, I don't know. I didn't really remember him,' she confessed truthfully, trying to explain her mixed emotions.

'That's about what I would expect. But you felt comfortable, happy with him?'

'Oh, yes. I think I love him, but...'

'No buts. Obviously at some deeper level of your mind you do recognise him; just give it time. I must admit I've never seen a more devoted husband than Mr Zarcourt. To hire an air ambulance must have cost him a fortune.' He shook his head in amazement. 'You certainly have nothing to worry about.' He turned to leave, just as the door swung open and Conan walked in.

Josie's eyes skimmed over him, registering the sombre business suit, and the silk shirt and tie that went with it.

He looked hard and arrogant, and, recalling her own reflection, she felt a sinking feeling in the pit of her stomach. How on earth had she managed to marry such a powerful-looking man? And what was this about an air ambulance?

'Josie.' He strode towards her. 'How are you today?' and bending over her, he brushed the hair from her brow. 'Black and blue but not so swollen.' He eyed the bruise on her face clinically as if he were the doctor.

'Apart from having no memory, I'm fine!' she said dryly, colour flaring in her cheeks at the touch of his hand on her brow.

'Is she?' he asked bluntly, glancing in the direction of the doctor. 'She looks a little flushed.'

'I was just telling your wife she's going to make a full recovery, but I would like to keep her under observation for a few days. She needs a bit of reassurance with her temporary loss of memory.'

'How temporary?' Conan demanded hardily. 'A day? A week?'

'One can't say with this kind of thing.' Dr Ferguson gestured with his hands. 'It could be five minutes, or five months. As I told you yesterday, time and patience and no forcing the issue is all your wife needs. Now, if you will excuse me, I have my rounds to complete.'

'So, you need reassurance, according to the doctor. Is that true?' Conan asked when they were alone.

'I don't know, but the doctor said something about an air ambulance. What exactly happened?' she demanded, sitting up in bed in agitation, sure Conan was not telling her the whole story.

'Your accident was at our place in the country. You spent a day in a local hospital, then I arranged to have you flown down to this clinic.'

'So I was out for three days, then?' She watched him carefully but he avoided her gaze.

'More like a week, but it's all over now so stop worrying.'

But she could not help worrying. Exactly how long had she been out? She sat up straighter in the bed, about to challenge him, when she felt her baby kick, and unthinkingly grabbed Conan's hand.

'Quick, the baby moved.' She felt his resistance for an instant, and then his large hand splayed over her stomach. She glanced up at him and caught the oddest expression in his dark eyes, then, as the baby kicked again, a look of total surprise and wonder.

'My God! Does it hurt?' he demanded, snatching his hand away.

'No, of course not.' Josie suddenly felt very foolish; she had the fleeting notion that even though Conan said he was her husband, and they were having a child, they had never been very close. 'How long have we been married?' she suddenly asked.

Conan sat down on the side of the bed and took her hand in his, his eyes fixed on her hand lying over her stomach. He twisted the rings around on her finger. 'We were married last year—a quiet wedding, after a whirlwind romance.'

'A whirlwind romance!' Josie exclaimed, in disbelief. 'You don't look the type to rush into anything.'

'That's true. I was a very staid banker until I met you.' His deep voice softened. 'But I took one look at you and knew I had to have you. Fate, kismet, call it what you will.' He held her hand, his dark eyes roaming lovingly over her small face. 'You have been with me ever since,' he drawled huskily. 'In mind and body. You are my wife; never doubt it.' And, lifting her hand to his lips, he kissed her slender fingers one by one. Watching her carefully he folded her hand in his and, leaning forward, pressed his lips to her mouth.

Josie's lips parted, their breath mingling, and she sighed with pleasure. Her body remembered him instantly, and the passion of his kiss knocked every thought out of her head.

'That's better,' Conan declared some time later, his dark eyes gleaming with sensual amusement. 'I can't wait to get you home and in my bed.'

Josie flushed vividly at his suggestive comment and tried to ease away from him. He touched her and she melted, but with no memory of the past she felt a bit like how she imagined a virgin must feel on her wedding night. It was stupid, she knew, but the sense of fear made her wary.

Sitting back, Conan smiled. 'Have I told you how lovely you look today?' With one long finger he traced the scooped outline of her nightdress over the soft curve of her breasts and back again, the knuckles of his other fingers grazing across her nipples.

Warmth spread right through her body, her breasts hardening at his seductive touch, her nipples clearly outlined against the fine silk fabric. 'Please, you're embarrassing me,' she murmured. 'Someone might come in.'

He threw his head back with a great shout of laughter. 'Oh, Josie, you're priceless. You're my wife, and pregnant, and you still blush like a rose when I touch you.' Dropping his hand, he shook his head in mock exasperation.

At the word 'rose', she remembered his flowers of that morning. 'I forgot to thank you for the roses,' she said quickly, glad of the chance to change the subject.

But it did not work as Conan responded. 'So thank me properly—a kiss might do it!' He grinned wickedly, his dark eyes daring her to accept the challenge.

Her own eyes mirrored her uncertainty. But why not? she asked herself. Any husband would expect as much, and Conan was her husband. There was something in the air between them—the familiar sensation, the glimmer of recognition she had experienced last night, appeared to be growing stronger in her mind every time she saw him.

'Does it really take so much thinking about?' Conan demanded, his gaze direct and serious. 'I have gone through hell the past few days, imagining I might lose you. I could do with some reassurance myself.'

He was right. She had been so tied up in her own worries, she had never given a thought to how he must feel. The doctor had told her he'd haunted the hospital when she was unconscious, driving the staff half crazy with his constant questions.

'Conan.' She murmured his name, and reaching out, she clasped his broad shoulders. Stretching up to him, she put her mouth to his. His lips were firm and warm as, gently, she discovered the shape of them with her tongue. She felt them soften beneath her caressing touch and gradually she increased the pressure of her mouth on his and felt his response. It was exciting to be in control, she realised. 'Conan,' she repeated, and in that instant any last doubt vanished. He was her husband. Instinctively she knew they loved each other. She would never have dared kiss him so blatantly otherwise.

Her eyes flew open as in one swift movement he lowered her back against the pillows, and followed her down. He gently cradled her head in his hands, his handsome face flushed, his pupils dilated, black with desire, reflecting she knew the longing in her own.

'My darling, darling Josie. You can't know how long I've waited for this.' He groaned, his mouth claiming hers in a kiss of tender possession. 'You're mine, all mine,' he declared huskily, his lips hot against the pulse that beat madly in her throat. He went lower, nuzzling at her firm breasts through the fine silk of her nightgown. Somehow he pushed the fabric down, and she felt his breath on her naked breasts.

Her eyes widened in shocked pleasure, her body trembling at his intimate caress. She gasped, and closed her eyes against the powerful surge of emotion that swept through her as he drew the tip of her breast into the burning heat of his mouth.

She didn't hear the nurse; it was only when Conan suddenly sat up and swiftly tucked the sheet around her shoulders that she was aware of Ann's presence.

'Sorry to interrupt, Mr Zarcourt, but I did knock. Dinner is served in five minutes.' Ann walked out, grinning as she went.

Josie, her body aching with frustration, glanced up at Conan and saw the same frustration mirrored in the depths of his dark eyes.

'I should have my head examined, never mind yours.' His lips twisted in a rueful smile. 'Sorry, Josie, but I couldn't help myself. I only have to look at you to want you. I know that's no excuse.' He ran his fingers through his hair. 'I should have remembered you're ill—the accident and all the complications.'

Her overheated body turned quickly cold at the word 'complications'. 'What complications?' she blurted. Was there something the doctor wasn't telling her? 'Our baby...?'

'No, no, nothing like that, Josie. You and the baby are fine; a few more days and you can come home. By complications I meant the nurse walking in when I was trying to make love to my wife.'

'It was embarrassing,' Josie admitted, suddenly feeling shy, and she was grateful when the door opened, putting an end to the conversation. It was the auxiliary nurse with the dinner trolley.

Conan stood up, and leant over to kiss her gently on the lips. 'It won't happen again until I get you home,' he murmured. 'I must leave now but I'll be back tomorrow—and stop worrying.' he admonished. 'A few days ago I thought I'd lost you, but now we have a lifetime ahead of us. What's a little memory loss against that?'

Today was the day... Conan would be arriving any second to take her home. A home she still could not remember, however hard she tried. She was nervous, afraid of the world outside her hospital room. She was being stupid, she knew; the doctor had reassured her, as had Conan, but she couldn't help it...

Josie glanced once more in the mirror, and adjusted the collar of her coat. It was a lovely outfit: a jade-green cashmere dress, with a high roll neck and cut to flare gently from her bust, with a matching coat that hung cape-like in deep folds almost to her ankles. She had asked Conan if it was new, and he had laughed and said. 'Of course; what did you expect when you're expanding by the week?'

Affronted by his comment, she had not questioned his explanation. One thing Josie had learned over the past four days was that her husband was a master at avoiding a direct question. The house in the country where she had been staying when she had had the accident was a case in point. She had asked him to describe it to her and his answer had been that it was being renovated so there was no point. He had visited her every day, and they'd talked on a variety of subjects. He was a brilliant and amusing conversationalist, yet after he'd left at night and she'd had time to think Josie had realised that he'd carefully evaded any attempt she'd made to discuss the past. She'd told herself he was probably following Dr Ferguson's orders, but for some reason it made her uneasy.

'Ready and waiting? Just how I like my women!'

Josie's heart leapt at the sound of Conan's voice, and she spun around to face him. He was wearing a camel-coloured overcoat that fitted perfectly across his wide shoulders. He looked wonderful, and all her nagging doubts vanished, to be replaced with a delicious lightness of heart.

'Women, plural! How many women do you have, husband mine?' she asked mockingly.

Stepping forward, he put an arm around her shoulder and led her towards the door. 'Sadly, none,' he said, but the wickedly sensual gleam in his dark eyes belied his mournful tone. 'You see, I have this beautiful, pregnant, sexy wife, who unfortunately crashed her car, and I've been ill with frustration for ages, but I'm hopeful of a cure very soon. What do you think of my chances?' he queried, tongue-in-cheek.

Josie burst out laughing. 'You're an idiot!'

'I must be to keep you talking here when I could be halfway home with you by now,' he said huskily, and, swooping down, he kissed her.

The first thing that hit Josie was the noise.

'London is a bit of a shock to the nervous system for anyone, Josie, so don't be afraid,' Conan commanded softly, and, opening the passenger door of a gleaming black BMW, he saw her safely inside and fastened her seat belt. 'There now; you're safe,'

It was uncanny how he could sense her every thought. He was right, she *was* frightened, she thought as she watched him walk around the front of the car and slip into the driving seat.

'Am I so obvious?' she asked, shooting him a sidelong glance.

'Not to anyone else, no.' He started the car and guided it out of the car park. 'You look the picture of cool, calm, beautiful womanhood.' He smiled briefly at her. 'But then I know you intimately,' he concluded huskily.

Josie looked away from the sensual gleam in his eyes, the drawling inflection of his last comment causing a flicker of fear in her mind. Covertly she watched him as he guided the car through the chaotic city traffic. In profile his face looked sterner somehow, almost arrogant. She bit her lower lip nervously. After all, he was still a stranger to her. In the hospital, with other people around, she had tried to ignore the fact she did not remember him. Amnesia must be the loneliest illness in the world. She had been happy just to know she belonged to someone.

As she sat next to him, aware of his every movement, of the strength of his large hands manipulating the car through the horrendous traffic, it hit Josie forcibly how dependent she and her unborn child were on Conan—for the past, the present, and the future. It was an unsettling feeling, and one she vaguely resented.

'We've arrived.'

She jumped at the sound of his voice. She'd been so engrossed in her own troubled thoughts, she hadn't noticed the car stopping. Climbing out of the car, she looked up at the elegant Georgian terrace house. It was lovely but she had no memory of it.

Conan took her arm and led her up the short flight of stone steps. 'Our home.'

Josie cast him a puzzled glance. He seemed almost triumphant, but quickly her attention was diverted as the door swung open and a grizzled old man beamed at them.

'Good evening, sir. Madam.'

'Cut out the act, Jeffrey,' Conan commanded, with a grin. 'You haven't the face for a formal butler—or the accent.' Turning to Josie, he ushered her into the house. 'This is Jeffrey. Ring any bells?'

'No.' She faced the broadly smiling little man. 'I'm sorry, Jeffrey.'

'No need to apologise, Josie. I'm so glad to see you home where you belong—and you look better than ever,' he told her, still grinning.

Josie immediately warmed to him. She had no memory of him but it did not seem to matter and her answering smile was equally broad. 'Thank you, Jeffrey.'

Conan reached out and began unfastening the buttons of her coat.

'You'll be glad to know your accident achieved what I've been trying to achieve for years. That is to persuade Jeffrey to live here. As soon as he heard of your accident he insisted on moving in to the attic rooms.' He slipped her coat from her shoulders and handed it to the man in question. 'Jeffrey reckons he's an expert on amnesia, along with pregnant women and everything else. He told me quite firmly that you cannot be left alone. When I'm at work he will be with you all the time, and act as your chauffeur. No more driving at present.'

'I'm not sure I can drive,' Josie quipped.

'Sensible girl.' Conan grinned. 'Stay that way and let Jeffrey show you to our room. You need a rest before dinner. I have some work to do.'

The room Jeffrey took her to was huge and elegant, with a massive double bed that seemed to dominate the room. Off it was a bathroom and a smaller dressing room with a stripped-down single bed that did not look as if it had been used in years. Josie walked back into the centre of the bedroom as Jeffrey reappeared with her suitcase.

'Would you like me to unpack for you?'

'No, no, I can do that.'

'A cup of tea, then? Anything at all?' he asked.

'No, thank you. I think I might just have a rest, and then a bath.'

'Excellent idea, Josie. You must take good care of yourself and the baby—and can I just say how happy I am about the little one?'

Long after Jeffrey had left, Josie lay on the bed, trying to sleep, but was unable to do so. Her mind spun with unanswered questions. Her accident had only been a week or so ago. So how come Jeffrey had not known earlier she was pregnant? She rubbed her swollen stomach tenderly; it must have been pretty obvious. And why, as a pregnant married lady, did the thought of sharing this admittedly luxurious bed with Conan make her feel so apprehensive? She must have made love to him dozens of times before. She had the bump to prove it...

Finally she slipped into a restless sleep, eventually waking to find it was almost dark, with the sound of running water coming from the bathroom. The sound surprised her into sitting up—Jeffrey must have left a tap running. Sliding her feet to the floor, she padded in stockinged feet across to the bathroom door, opened it and walked in. She came to an abrupt halt, her eyes widening to their fullest extent.

'Sorry, did I disturb you?'

'Disturb' did not begin to do justice to the way Josie felt. Conan, obviously having just stepped out of the shower, was standing stark naked in the middle of the room, briskly rubbing his hair with a towel. Her fascinated gaze slid down over his wide shoulders, the broad chest matted with black curls that arrowed down over his flat stomach and bushed out at the junction of his legs. Words failed her at the sight of his manhood, his lean hips and long, tanned, well-shaped legs. Beads of water glistened on his bronzed skin, and she could not tear her eyes away.

'You're beautiful,' she finally murmured. How could she have forgotten such a perfect specimen of masculinity? she wondered.

'I think that's my line, Josie,' he said with a husky chuckle, and, walking towards her, he casually wrapped the towel he had been drying his hair with around his hips.

Not before time, Josie thought, swallowing hard; she was in danger of having a heart attack. Glancing up at his smiling face, she turned scarlet. 'Sorry. I...I thought a tap was...' She stopped when she realised she was stammering like an idiot.

'You have seen me naked before, Josie, I can assure you.' And, placing his hands on her shoulders, he swooped down and kissed her open mouth. Then, grinning, he straightened up, lightly squeezed her shoulders, and let her go.

'I didn't mean to wake you, Josie, but I needed a shower and a shave before dinner. Will you come down for dinner, or would you prefer to eat up here?'

'No. Yes. I—I'll come downstairs,' she stammered, and shot back into the bedroom, closing the door behind her.

To her relief Conan did not follow her, but she heard him go into the dressing room. Of course! Where else would he keep his clothes?

Her own clothes, she discovered, when she began unpacking her suitcase, were in the large wardrobe in the bedroom. She eyed the contents and sighed. Nothing jolted her memory; in fact they all looked new. But then why shouldn't they? They were all loose-fitting or maternity clothes.

She made her way downstairs and immediately Jeffrey appeared, and he showed her into the dining room. Like the rest of the house it had a comfortable feel about it, though elegant and totally in keeping with the Georgian era. But still not familiar. She frowned.

'Stop it, Josie; you'll end up with a line between your eyes. Remember what the doctor said? No forcing the issue.' Conan strode into the room, and pulled out a chair for her. 'Sit down, stop worrying and eat.'

'Yes, oh, master!' she joked as he sat in the chair at the top of the table with Josie on his right-hand side.

Jeffrey served their meal—broccoli soup, then fresh

poached salmon, both of which he insisted was good for pregnant mums.

Josie accepted the salmon Jeffrey offered her with a wrinkle of her nose, then flushed as she saw the amused lift of Conan's eyebrow. 'Excuse him, Josie; I'm sure Jeffrey thinks he is having the baby!'

'That *would* be a miracle,' she smiled, and some of the tension eased from her body. 'But I don't think I like salmon,' she concluded—but put a forkful in her mouth anyway. She chewed for a moment. 'Actually it's quite nice. Obviously I can't trust my own instinct.' And she ate the rest without comment.

The pudding she did refuse, simply because she felt full. But she watched Conan devour a generous portion of apple pie, smothered in cream, and wondered how he kept so hard and lean. A vivid image of his naked body flashed into her mind, which was enough to set her pulse racing, and hastily she picked up her glass of water and finished it off. Suddenly the thought of the night ahead loomed large in her mind. She had no excuse for not sharing the marital bed. The baby maybe? But she didn't think so; the doctor had made a point of telling her, along with a lot of other advice, that sex was perfectly safe. She really had to get over this childish fear of intimacy with her husband.

Conan suggested coffee in the drawing room and Josie agreed. She sat down on the sofa and Conan joined her, casually putting an arm around her. Curved as she was against his side, her head resting against his broad chest, the steady rise and fall of his deep breathing lulled her into a deep sense of security.

Jeffrey walked in and set the coffee tray on the occasional table, and said goodnight.

Josie smiled her thanks, and unthinkingly placed her hand on Conan's thigh to push herself up into a sitting position. 'Shall I pour?' She threw him a glance, and caught a flare of desire in the darkening depths of his eyes. She felt his muscles flex and tense beneath her palm, and she was belatedly aware of the intimacy of the situation.

She snatched her hand back. 'Sugar, milk?' she asked, edging away from him, suddenly hit by an attack of nerves.

'Black, one sugar.'

Keeping her attention fixed on the tray, she filled two cups and handed one to Conan. She picked up her own, drained it in one gulp and jumped to her feet.

'I'm going to bed, if you don't mind. It has been a long day and I'm tired.'

Conan rose to his feet. 'Of course,' he agreed, with a sardonic glance down at her flushed face 'I have a few telephone calls to make. I'll be up later.'

Josie dashed out of the room, sure he had guessed how nervous she felt. Standing in the bathroom twenty minutes later, fresh from a shower Josie surveyed her naked body with a grim smile. While rubbing baby oil on to her tummy, she remembered Conan's magnificent nudity earlier, and decided ruefully that she had nothing to worry about. Conan was hardly likely to be overcome with passion for a small round person. Even if he did love her.

'Here, let me help you do that.'

She spun around, her eyes widening on Conan's serious face. Lost in her own thoughts, she had not heard him enter. Her instinctive reaction was to hide her nakedness from his intent gaze, but something in his expression stopped her. He was openly studying the soft fullness of her breasts, and she shivered as he stepped forward and took the bottle of oil from her unresisting grasp.

'I'm getting fat,' she blurted—the first thing that came into her head.

'No, Josie. You're a ripe, voluptuous woman, and I adore you,' he said huskily.

Josie trembled. He was so close she could smell the cool,

masculine scent of him; something quivered in her belly, and it was not their child...

'Come.' He lowered his head and brushed her lips with his. 'I can do this better in the bedroom.'

He was her husband, and he had the right, but none of that mattered to Josie. The simple truth was, she wanted this man. She made no effort to stop him as he gently lifted her into his arms and, cradling her against his broad chest carried her into the room, placing her in the middle of the wide bed. She reached for the sheet, but Conan stopped her.

'No, Josie, darling; let me look at you.' Sitting down on the bed, he poured some oil direct from the bottle on to her stomach. Then, reaching over, he placed the bottle on the bedside table.

At the first touch of his large hands on her stomach she quivered, then, as he gently massaged the oil over the mound that kept their child safe, she began to relax.

'You must have done this before,' she whispered, her eyes closing, relaxing at the soothing stroke of his hands on her distended stomach.

'And much, much more,' he said softly, his hands leaving her stomach and stroking up under her breasts.

Her eyes flew open and clashed with the gleaming dark gold of his. 'Conan?' she queried as his hands inched higher, cupping her breasts, his long fingers massaging the firm flesh. She moaned as his touch filled her with delicious pleasure.

'More oil, I think,' he drawled. 'And a little less clothing.' Wide-eyed and breathless, she watched as he stood up and shrugged out of his clothes. Once naked, he picked up the bottle of oil and slowly, deliberately trickled a drop of liquid onto the hardened peaks of her breasts.

For a long moment he stared down at her, drinking in her beauty with glittering eyes. While Josie fought down a brief flutter of fear at the sight of his massive aroused male body, at the same time her body ached for his caress. He lowered himself down on the bed beside her, and when he finally touched her she shuddered all over.

His dark eyes gleaming with the banked-down fire of passion, his hands swept slowly down over her stomach and thighs in a long, smooth motion, then up again, his palms lingering on her stomach and then sliding up to her breasts.

Josie gasped as he bent over her. His mouth capturing her parted lips, he kissed her. His fingers smoothed the oil into her breasts, his thumb gently massaging the hard tip, and still he kissed her, his tongue plunging deep in her mouth. She touched him, hesitantly at first, letting her hands slide over his shoulders. She felt him shudder and realised the control he was exerting over himself.

His dark head moved from her mouth to her throat and his hair tickled softly against her chin as he moved lower. Then the feel of his tongue, warm and wet, encircling one taut nipple, sent tremors through every part of her.

Conan lifted his head, his eyes heavy-lidded with desire. 'More oil or...?' The question simmered on the air as his hands stroked down over her stomach once more and lower to her thighs, the oil long since absorbed, although still he massaged her sensitive flesh.

'Conan?' she murmured. 'How could I have forgotten?' She trailed her hands down his back and lower over his buttocks. 'You feel so right.'

It was the sign he was waiting for. Conan's head swooped down and their mouths met and fused. He teased her with long, drugging kisses, his fingers slipping between her legs which were parted and ready for him.

Josie writhed beneath him, her oil-slicked body sliding against his naked flesh as his fingers found the secret centre of her. Then his mouth found the peak of her breast and gently he took the engorged nipple between his teeth. Her body was on fire. Her hands grasped his head and tangled in his thick dark hair, but still he turned his head and subjected her other breast to the same sweet torment, and all the time his seeking, teasing fingers brought her to new heights of pleasure, until the pleasure became one burning, aching need.

He lifted his head. His eyes had narrowed to slits, and the flesh was taut across his high cheekbones. 'I don't want to hurt you, Josie.' His hands slid across to grasp her thighs, holding her firmly against the mattress, and he pushed down on her, allowing her to feel the full extent of his arousal. 'But I can't wait much longer,' he murmured, flicking both her breasts with his tongue in a sensuous reminder.

'Touch me—show me you want me,' he rasped.

Want him! She would die if she did not have him, and, sliding one hand down his long body, she curled her fingers around him.

His great body shuddered, and he guided her hand against his body, his mouth hard as he caught hers in a deep, hungry kiss, and Josie responded with equal fervour, the wonder of him filling her mind with a joy so profound, she could not understand how it was possible she had forgotten him.

If Josie had ever had any inhibitions she certainly did not now. They touched tenderly, discovering and delighting in their mutual passion, the tension stretching almost to pain, until Conan rolled over on his back and, positioning her astride him, pulled her down towards him and suckled on her breast as he thrust up into her ready warmth.

She clenched around him and within seconds his great body was bucking against her, driving her over the edge to a shattering climax as his hot seed spilled inside her, and she heard his deep growl of release. She lay sprawled across his chest, still joined to him, as eddying circles of pleasure feathered from her innermost being.

'Are you all right?' The words seemed to rumble from his chest.

Josie lifted her head and folded her arms across his heaving chest to look down into his face.

'Awestruck,' she breathed, her eyes clinging to his own, which were narrowed and black with passion. 'I feel as though I have just discovered the meaning of life, love and all that.' A lazy smile curved her love-swollen lips. Resting on one arm, she used her other hand to brush his damp hair from his brow in a tender gesture of love, not taking her eyes from his flushed face. 'I can't believe I forgot this.' She moved her hips restlessly against him, and gasped as she felt him swelling inside her.

'Give me a minute and I'll remind you again,' Conan drawled, his arms wrapping firmly around her, holding her pressed to his heart.

'Is it always like this between us?' she asked, gently nibbling on his chin, and she did not see his eyes narrow with grim determination.

'Always, and for ever. Now stop talking and let me show you again,' Conan growled, and rolled her beneath him. Leaning on his elbows with his hands cradling her head, he began to move gently inside her, while he sipped at her mouth and breasts in a long, lazy loving that ended in the same breathtaking climax.

CHAPTER NINE

JOSIE'S eyes fluttered open. It was dark and warm, she was snuggled against the side of a very large man, and she was dying to go to the lavatory. Very gently, she wriggled a little down the bed to escape the long arm that curved around her shoulder.

Carefully she raised herself up on one elbow and looked down at her sleeping husband. His dark hair was tousled, his long lashes curled against his cheeks. He looked younger and somehow vulnerable. Josie's heart squeezed with love for him, and carefully, so as not to wake him, she slid off the bed.

Naked, she padded to the bathroom, and a few moments later she picked her nightdress off the rail and slipped it on before returning to the bedroom.

'Josie,' Conan's voice greeted her. He sat up in bed, and switched on the bedside light. His sleep-hazed gaze searched urgently around the room, until he saw her walking towards him 'What...? Where have you been?' he demanded, his dark eyes skimming over her face and down over the long white cotton nightdress that covered her small frame.

Josie was wide awake, and chuckled at his bemused expression. 'The call of nature beckoned. According to Dr Masters, one of the down sides of pregnancy is the urge to go to the bathroom more often. Apparently it depends on the way the baby is lying,' she told him chattily as she walked across the room and climbed back into bed. 'Sorry I woke you.'

'Oh.' Conan reached out and pulled her into the circle

of his arms. 'You gave me a fright. I thought you were a ghost, in this thing.' He plucked at the pristine white cotton enveloping her. Switching off the light, he turned her in his arms and leant over her to kiss her eyes, and nose, and lips.

'Again,' she murmured teasingly against his mouth, her slender arm curving around his neck.

'You're insatiable, woman!' He chuckled and slid his hand down her thigh and up under her nightdress, quickly removing the offending garment.

A long time later Josie lay against him, tired but curious. 'Conan?' She murmured his name.

'Go to sleep,' he rasped. 'It takes the male of the species a little longer to recover than the female; I need a rest.'

'No, not that.' She nuzzled his neck. 'But I was wondering. Have I ever done this with anyone else?' She could not imagine she had shared such bliss with anyone other than Conan. 'I can't believe I have but I don't know.' His arm tightened around her, and she felt a brief tension in his hard body.

'You were a virgin when we first met,' he stated emphatically.

'I'm glad.' She sighed deeply, snuggling into him. 'I might have lost my memory, but I knew you were my soul mate,' she murmured, and in minutes was asleep.

But if she had seen the expression on Conan's face she would not have slept so trustingly.

'The March wind will blow and we will have snow.' Josie murmured the proverb to herself as she gazed idly out of the drawing-room window, watching the snowflakes dance past and fall gently to the ground. She stirred restlessly on the sofa as the baby gave her a mighty kick. Usually the feel of their child moving inside her brought a smile to her lips, but not today.

For the past couple of weeks she had lived with a constant sense of foreboding. She'd told herself it was just nerves. Tonight she was hosting her first dinner party since her accident, but as far as her memory was concerned it was the first dinner party of her life. A wry smile twisted her lips; her inability to remember was preying heavily on her mind. Resting her head back against the sofa, she closed her eyes against the nagging pain behind them, and let the events of the past few weeks run through her mind.

After the first evening back from the hospital, when she had shared her husband's bed, Josie had been happy. Conan was a wonderful husband. Kind and attentive, he always attended the antenatal classes with her, cradling her head in his lap while she practised the breathing exercises. Her visits to the hospital were the same—Conan went with her; nothing was too much trouble for him. Every night without fail he delighted in massaging her swollen stomach with oil, and every night they fell asleep in each other's arms.

Life was perfect, except for her amnesia. Her brows drew together in a deep frown; she hated the word. But she was fast reaching the conclusion that Conan didn't care if she never recovered her memory. It was the only bone of contention between them. When she questioned him, he answered, but reluctantly, she could tell. His eyes avoided hers or he laughed off her queries. Lately she had caught him watching her quite a few times with a dark, brooding intensity that sent a chill down her spine. They did not make love quite so often, but when she challenged him he always gave her a glib excuse. One of his top executives was stuck in America, so Conan was working harder than usual. He was also concerned about the baby, or more often he was concerned about her; but none of the excuses quite rang true.

Josie bit her lip. Perhaps it was her over-active imagination, but she could sense something was troubling him. And last Saturday night had only added to her disquiet.

Every week Conan took her out to the theatre or to a film and dinner, or maybe they would go shopping. The room set aside for the nursery had been decorated, and they had happily chosen all the furnishings together. But last Saturday evening, after they returned from seeing a new musical, they had had their first real argument.

Lying on the sofa with Conan beside her, cradling her aching feet in his lap, she asked, 'Did you really enjoy the show?' It had been a very avant-garde type of musical.

He squeezed her toes. 'The lady in blue paint was quite explicit. Blue was definitely the colour for what she was doing,' he opined dryly.

'What was she doing?' Josie asked. As she remembered it, the woman simply had pranced around naked but for paint, with another woman in a black body stocking.

'If you don't know you're even more innocent than I thought,' Conan chuckled.

'Typical of a man—never answer a direct question. I'm sure a woman friend would have explained what the dance was all about and we would have had a good giggle.' The thought gave her pause, and, glancing at Conan, she added, 'Do I have any friends?'

With Jeffrey to watch over her and Conan to love her, Josie had not let herself think too much about her memory loss. Dr Ferguson had told her to carry on with her life, avoid stress, and allow her memory to return naturally.

'I don't know,' Conan said tersely. 'As I told you, ours was a whirlwind courtship; we met and married in weeks.'

'I know.' Josie sighed. 'You said I was born in London, but we met in the country, and my father moved in with yours when we married. I get postcards from both of them, they're obviously enjoying the cruise. It all seems so cosy, but I can't help feeling—'

'But nothing, Josie. Don't try and force yourself to remember, and anyway I thought I was enough for you,' he prompted flashing her a brief smile that did not quite reach his eyes.

'You are,' she quickly assured him. 'But I just wish I knew—'

'Stop it, Josie.' He cut her off again, and, placing her feet back on the sofa, he stood up.

'No,' she'd snapped back. 'It's all well and good for you to tell me not to try, but I'm sick of not knowing who and what I am. I spoke to Dr Ferguson yesterday, and he seems to think any day now I'll remember, but…' It was late, she was tired, and her hormones were haywire. 'I feel like a fat, useless lump, hidden away in the house to be trotted out on a Saturday like a child receiving a treat.' She sounded like a shrew, and she knew she was being unfair, but she didn't seem able to stop.

'You spoke to Dr Ferguson yesterday?' Conan enquired grimly. 'You had no appointment.'

'I telephoned.'

'You shouldn't have wasted his time; don't do it again.'

Her head shot back and she stared up at him. 'How dare you tell me what to do?' she cried, incensed by the anger in his tone. Her loving husband had a temper, it seemed, but so did she. 'I might be your wife but I am not a child to be told what to do—by you or anyone else.' She struggled to her feet and glared at him.

'No, but you are *with* child,' he shot back, and, as though he'd realised that his tone had upset her, he added quietly, 'And you are not fat, or useless. You're a beautiful, glowing girl, and my wife. So please don't excite yourself, Josie; it isn't good for you or the baby. I thought I was protecting you by keeping what are, after all, strangers to you from visiting. But if it will make you happy I'll invite a few mutual friends around for dinner next week.'

Josie should have been satisfied, but later, as she lay next to Conan in bed, tired in body and mind but unable to sleep, she felt a growing fear for the future. Conan had massaged her stomach as usual, and kissed her lightly, before turning over and going to sleep. But she had sensed a change in him, a mental distancing of himself from her. Eventually she did sleep, but her dreams were filled with weird pictures of an ultra-modern naked blue lady, plus ancient portraits of total strangers in costumes from the last century.

Thinking about it now, Josie realised she was still apprehensive, and she wished Conan would hurry up and get home. Their guests would be arriving in little more than two hours. Jeffrey was slaving away in the kitchen, having flatly refused her offer to assist him. Maybe if she had a bath, and tried to relax, she would feel better.

Later, bathed and seated on the bed, wearing a blue silk robe, Josie tried to brush the tangles from her hair.

'Here, let me do that.' Conan walked into the room, shedding his jacket and tossing it on to the bed. He sat down beside her, and took the brush from her hand to brush her long hair. 'How are you and Junior today?' he asked, dropping a light kiss on the exposed curve of her neck.

Josie shivered and smiled. 'Fine, now you're home,' she murmured. To see him was enough to make her happy.

'Good.' He stood up and grinned down at her. 'I see I'm too late to get you to share the shower. Pity...' His dark eyes glinted wickedly. 'But I'll catch you later.' And, swinging on his heel, he headed for the bathroom.

Josie grimaced at her reflection in the mirror. Her face and hair were fine; it was the rest that took some getting used to. She was twenty-seven weeks pregnant and there was no disguising her belly. Her red dress was from a designer maternity boutique. Slashed straight across her chest, exposing the curve of her breasts, the narrow straps supported the bodice, and the soft silk, cut on the bias, skimmed around her body, but could not hide her bump.

'You look beautiful.'

She hadn't heard Conan come in, but the feel of his long arm around her and his large hand splayed over their child brought a glimmer of a smile to her face. Her violet eyes captured his in the mirror. He was standing behind her, naked apart from a towel around his hips. His broad, tanned shoulders, gleaming in the artificial light, appeared to surround her protectively.

'Of course, you're not biased,' she teased. The one certainty in her life was her love for Conan and her unborn child, and her heart lurched as she saw his golden eyes darken, his hands stroking up to cup her breasts, her nipples tautening at his touch. She sighed. She felt the stirring of his masculine response against her buttocks, and for a long moment their eyes fused and reflected in the mirror a mutual need and desire. Conan blinked and abruptly let her go.

'I'm probably a lot of things you don't rem—realise,' he said curtly. 'But right now I had better get dressed; our guests will be arriving shortly.'

Josie watched him as he crossed to the bathroom, a worried frown marring her smooth brow. Something was bothering him. She gave a shrug; now was not the time for an in-depth discussion, and she went downstairs to check with Jeffrey that everything was ready. Walking out of the kitchen into the hall, she stopped as Conan ran lightly down the stairs. Her breath caught in her throat. He looked gorgeous in a dinner suit, but then he looked gorgeous in anything—or nothing, Josie thought with a secret smile.

'Remember this was your idea,' Conan murmured as the doorbell rang.

An hour later Josie was beginning to enjoy herself. The food was perfect: a light consommé followed by Dover sole, and the main course an invention of Jeffrey's—chicken breasts stuffed and cooked in his secret sauce, with all the accompanying vegetables.

They were ten at the table. Josie did not remember any of the guests but was immediately at ease, as Conan had apparently explained she was suffering from amnesia. Pamela, the small lady across the table from Josie, was delightful as was her husband and the bluff Mr. Smales and his wife, Betty. Martin and Belinda Bewick were a couple about Conan's age and full of stories about their three children. A tall blonde woman, Angela, was not quite so friendly, but her brother Steve, a strikingly handsome American, more than made up for her, keeping Josie amused with his stories.

By the time they all retired to the drawing room, Josie was feeling quite relaxed and her headache from earlier had eased slightly. Pamela and Belinda had promised to call around to see her without their husbands, to arrange a shopping trip. It was only when Pamela excused herself to go to the bathroom that Josie felt a twinge of disquiet. Angela turned her cold blue eyes on Josie and smiled with saccharine sweetness.

'I know it's hard in your condition to walk around,' she said, making Josie feel like a beached whale. 'But I'm dying to see what you've done to the nursery.' Angela stood up and, with a brief glance around the room before smiling down at Josie, she added, 'I'm sure the others won't mind—unless the stairs are too much for you?'

'No, no, of course not.' Josie got to her feet. 'I'll be delighted to show you,' she murmured, and led the way out of the room and up the stairs.

The nursery was next door to their bedroom, and Josie opened the door and stepped back as Angela marched past her and spun around to face her.

Josie glanced around the room and crossed to the muslin-draped crib, tenderly running her hand along the side. The room was perfect, with pale walls stencilled with a multitude of nursery rhymes. 'As you can see we chose pale lemon…'

'Drop the act,' Angela snapped.

Josie's head shot up. 'I beg your pardon?'

The hard blue eyes fixed on Josie seemed to pierce her brain, and a dull ache behind her eyes blurred her vision for a moment. She blinked, but Angela was still staring at her, very tall and dressed in a plain white gown. A brief image of the same woman dressed in black flickered in Josie's mind. Her subconscious was playing tricks, perhaps, but she had a nasty premonition it was more than that.

'You heard. I hate to admit it, Josie, but I almost admire you. I really thought it was that wholesome, innocent look of yours that had captured Con's fleeting interest, but you are much cleverer than I gave you credit for.'

'Cleverer?' What was the woman getting at?

'Yes, fancy catching a man like Con with the oldest trick in the book. When I got back last week and he told me you were suffering from amnesia, I didn't believe it for a second.'

'I don't know what you mean,' Josie said curtly, disliking the woman's abbreviation of her husband's name to Con. It smacked of a familiarity between the two of them she did not want to contemplate.

'Oh, come on,' Angela sneered. 'I was in New York when I heard of your accident, and I rang the office. Good manners dictated I ask after my boss's wife. But a very chatty secretary told me all about your accident. It was a simple calculation—married at the end of October but over five months pregnant.'

Josie gasped, and for a second her heart stopped beating.

'The amnesia was a brilliant touch; now you can pretend it never happened. Knowing what a soft touch Con is, he wouldn't dare mention it in your tender state of health,' she scoffed. 'My God, the child probably isn't even his.'

Josie looked at the other woman, the blood draining from her face, her hands clenching the edge of the crib in a death-grip. 'I don't know what you're talking about,' she managed to say between gritted teeth. 'But I think it's time we rejoined the others.'

'Bravo,' Angela jeered. 'You're quite an actress. I can't say I blame you. I might have tried it myself when I lived here with Con, except I can't stand kids; they're death to the figure.' She strolled past Josie, giving her a disparaging glance. 'But in your case it probably doesn't matter.' And she walked out.

Josie followed Angela down the stairs and back into the drawing room, her mind in turmoil. Her husband had lived with this woman! Why was she surprised? She did not know her own past, let alone Conan's! When she had first seen him in the hospital, she had wondered at her own good fortune to have such a dynamic, handsome husband. Only a fool would imagine he had reached his thirties without a few lovers, and Josie was the fool.

She looked at Conan as she walked into the room, but sat down next to Pamela, the pain in her head intensifying by the minute. Conan had only married her because she was pregnant, according to Angela. How could that be? she asked herself. They loved each other. She glanced at Conan again; his dark eyes were narrowed enquiringly on her face.

'All right, darling?' The endearment fell so easily from his lips.

'Yes, fine.' She forced her lips into a travesty of a smile, but she wasn't fine; she was dying inside.

Joe Smales began to tell a joke, and everyone spoke at once. 'No more shaggy-dog stories.'

Pamela stood up and smiled down at Josie. 'You know it's time to leave when Joe starts his famous—or infamous—jokes.'

Josie was struck by a sense of *déjà vu*. But was it...?

Suddenly a stabbing pain behind her eyes made her wince in agony as a thousand memories bombarded her mind. She vaguely registered everyone was standing up to leave.

'Are you sure you're all right?' Conan murmured, leaning over her and offering her his hand. She looked at him, so suave and sophisticated, and apparently concerned.

'I'm fine,' she repeated, ignoring his hand, her stomach churning as she rose to her feet to escort their guests out. Pamela and her husband departed with a smile, and a promise to call. While Josie, bile blocking her throat, prayed silently, Don't let me be sick, not yet.

She never knew how she made it upstairs to the bathroom. Then she was hanging over the toilet being violently sick, retching until her throat ached. She heard Conan banging on the door, his deep voice full of concern, but she did not answer him. The pain behind her eyes had intensified to such a degree she could hardly bear it, but the pain in her heart was infinitely worse.

She wanted to rant and rave at the trick Conan had played on her. How could she have been so stupid? After the accident she had grabbed at him the way a drowning man clutched a life-raft. Endlessly pouring out her love for him. Glorying in their lovemaking, wantonly eager to please him. Oh! And he had taught her the most intimate sensual pleasures, encouraging her to explore every sexy inch of him. When all the time he'd known the truth. They had never had a real marriage...

'Open this damn door,' she heard Conan yell, but she ignored him.

Josie wanted to weep but her eyes remained stubbornly dry. How conceited she had been, how confident. When she had wondered about her past, it had never once entered her head that Conan had married her for any other reason but love. Looking back over the past ten weeks, the passionate nights and sometimes days in his arms, he had never actually said he loved her. She groaned out loud in her agony and humiliation. Why should he? She had been his half-brother's first. Charles... Charles was the father of her child. How could she have forgotten?

The tears rolled unnoticed down her cheeks as she recalled the true circumstances of her marriage. A lot of little incidents suddenly made sense: Conan's careful avoidance of the past, while he moulded her to be his willing wife. But why? The question echoed in her brain. He'd married her to get Beeches Manor, but that had been settled at Christmas. He had had no real reason to see her again once he had the estate. He was a very wealthy, attractive man; he could have any woman he wanted, and he certainly had Angela.

Why? Why had he pretended to want her? There was no excuse for taking her to his bed, allowing her to think they had always had a passionate relationship, pretending to be the father of her child... Then she remembered. Conan had said once that his chief executive was held up in America. Of course. Angela had been in New York for two months. Josie had been a convenient body in the swine's bed, in the absence of his lover...

A loud crash had her jumping to her feet. The bathroom door hung off its hinges and Conan stood in the opening.

'Josie, darling...' he said, concern lacing his tone, then he stopped. His dark eyes searched her tear-drenched face, and something in her expression made him catch his breath.

Her violet eyes clashed with his. 'How could you?' Her voice broke on a sob.

'You've remembered, haven't you?'

He looked so cool, so calm that Josie wanted to scratch his eyes out; instead she lurched to the vanity unit and, turning on the tap, splashed her tear-stained face with cold water, then bent lower to drink some. Her head was pounding, her eyes stinging, and she could not bear to look at Conan.

'Josie.' His hand closed over her shoulder. 'Josie, darling, take it easy. You're in shock.'

She shrugged his hand off her shoulder and staggered out of the bathroom. Shock…? Was that what he called it, when her whole life was exposed as a lie?

'Please, Josie, lie down; I'll call the doctor.' Conan followed her into the bedroom.

Josie spun around to face him, her violet eyes flashing fury. 'No doctor, not yet. Why? Tell me why you lied to me,' she cried. 'Why did you let me think the baby was yours? What kind of sick pleasure did you get from fooling me?'

'It was hardly the time to tell you. You were unconscious in hospital for a week, or have you forgotten?' he bit out grimly, and, pulling at the tie at his throat, he flung off his jacket and shirt. 'And now is not the time to talk about it. You're tired, you've had a shock and you're not thinking straight.'

'But I am thinking straight, for the first time in months,' Josie snapped. 'No thanks to you. And I'm leaving.' She headed for the door, the only thought in her head to get as far away from Conan as possible. He caught her before she had taken two steps and swept her up in his arms, and deposited her firmly in the middle of the bed.

'Let go of me; let go,' she cried, but he was sprawled beside her, his hands holding her shoulders pinned to the bed.

'Stop it, Josie; you're becoming hysterical, and it can't be good for the baby.'

She stared up at him with anguished eyes. What did he care? It wasn't his baby, she thought bitterly, and opened her mouth to tell him so, but never got the chance.

'I know regaining your memory must be traumatic for

you, and I am prepared to make some allowances, but let's get one thing straight. *You are not going anywhere.* Is that clear?' he demanded hardily.

My, how magnanimous of him! He would make allowances for her. The gall of the man was unbelievable! Anger, ice-cold anger, surged through Josie. He was talking to her as if she were a six-year-old child, but then he had been doing that for months.

'As crystal, but you can't stop me, not any more,' she declared with as much force as she could muster—which wasn't a lot, she realised furiously, when she tried to sit up and ended up flat on her back on the bed with Conan lying half over her.

'Get off me, you great brute! I can't bear you to touch me!' she yelled.

'I don't remember you objecting to my touching you for the past few months—in fact quite the opposite. On more than one occasion you couldn't wait to get my clothes off.'

Her face burned at his mocking reminder, and she closed her eyes against the amusement she could see lurking in his. She was furious with herself at how easily he affected her, while he took her for a fool.

'Look at me, Josie,' he commanded.

She felt the warmth of his breath against her cheek and slowly opened her eyes. He was no longer amused; his handsome face was inches from her own and she shivered beneath the intensity of his gaze.

'You're pregnant, you're not thinking clearly, but if you will listen to me for a moment I can explain everything.'

But she did not want to. Bitterly, Josie realised Conan would have no trouble persuading her into his arms, lying beneath him, with his naked chest barely touching her breasts, his long leg hard against her side. Already she could feel the familiar weakness flooding through her, and she was never going down that route again. Calling up all her self-control, she forced herself to remain calm. 'Don't waste your time. We have nothing to say to each other. You tricked me, used me—'

'I never used you,' he cut in tautly. 'We are man and wife, and what we've shared for the past few weeks was a mutual passion. I'm not about to let you turn your back on everything—on us—for some stubborn misplaced pride.'

'Stubborn pride!' she spluttered. 'You have a nerve. I wasn't your wife. Ours was a marriage of convenience! Something you omitted to tell me when you were oh, so solicitous in the hospital!' she sneered. Did he take her for a complete idiot? He did not like her comment; she could tell by the tension in his long body. But he refused to be riled.

'I am not going to argue over the past, Josie. It has no relevance now. The important point is you *are* my wife in the fullest sense of the word, and when you have time to think about it you'll realise nothing has changed.'

'But everything has changed. You lied to me.'

'I never lied to you, my one sin, if you could call it that, was I omitted to tell you about your past, but only because I didn't want you to worry, in your delicate condition,' he said, his dark eyes shadowed with concern.

'Worry me!' she cried. His concern was not for her, she thought grimly. It was probably because his deviousness had been discovered. 'My God! Don't you think I'm worried now?' She couldn't stop herself. 'I lay on this bed with you. We made...' No, it had not been love, and that was where the real hurt lay, Josie recognised bitterly.

'Go on, say it,' Conan prompted. 'We made love.'

'It was only sex,' she spat out.

'If it was only sex, it was very good sex, and I have no intention of giving it up,' he drawled mockingly. His dark head lowered and his lips sought hers, and she turned her head away—anything to avoid his traitorous mouth.

'Come on, Josie.' he cajoled against her ear. 'If you were honest, you would admit you really don't want to leave me. You love how I make you feel. You know you do,' he declared, his thigh pressing into her as he slid his hands down her arms and back up in a seductive caress.

'No.' She pushed him, catching him unawares, and shot off the other side of the bed. Coldly, she turned to stare down at him sprawled on his back across the bed. His arrogance was only exceeded by his masculine conceit in his own powers of persuasion, she thought furiously.

'It's no good, Conan; I'm wise to you now, and I will never allow myself to be used by you again. Charles...' She got no further.

Conan leapt off the bed, his dark eyes shooting flames. 'I wondered when you'd get around to him,' he bit out, all pretence of caring gone. 'In that crazy head of yours you probably imagine you've been unfaithful to his memory.'

For a split second Josie thought she saw pain in his eyes. Then he hauled her into his arms. Ruthlessly his mouth ground down on hers, filled with rage and frustration. She was powerless to push him away; her hands were trapped between their bodies. She squirmed frantically in his iron grip, keeping her mouth firmly closed. Her fear of betraying her love for him and a burning sense of injustice gave her the strength to resist him. He lifted his head.

'That ploy won't work, Josie. You want me, not a dead man. I know you—two minutes on that bed and you'll be begging me for it,' he snarled.

Something snapped in Josie at his words. 'You don't know me at all!' she cried. 'You Zarcourt men are all the same—users and takers—and I wish I'd never set eyes on any of you.' Conan's hands dropped to his sides. The stunned expression on his face would have surprised Josie if she had noticed it, but she was too lost in her own hell, and everything she had kept bottled up for months came pouring out.

'First Charles got me drunk, or I would never have gone to bed with him. Then I found out I was pregnant.' Her eyes darkened with anguish as she relived the moment in her mind. 'Then you and your father used my condition for your own ends—the old man hoping to replace the son he had lost and you... You were worse. A plot of earth and bricks was your obsession.'

'No, Josie.' He reached out for her, and she slapped his hand away.

'Even my own father quite happily gave up our home at your instigation, and I, poor fool, was so ashamed, so confused. I let you all get away with it. But not any more. I'm finished with the lot of you.' It was true; she had had more than she could stand of lies and deceit. 'From now on it's going to be just me and my child, and the rest of you can go to hell!'

'Josie, stop. Don't get upset.' With his own temper firmly under control, Conan was trying to calm her down. 'You'll make yourself ill again.'

'And that would suit you just fine, because then you could lie to me some more, play the caring husband!' she raged.

'You're being ridiculous. I would never intentionally hurt you, you must know that!' he reasoned, once again reaching out to her.

She stepped back. 'I suppose pretending you and I had a normal marriage, when you knew I would find out the truth eventually, wasn't designed to hurt me,' she scoffed. 'Pretending to be the father of my child!'

Her last comment finally cracked his iron control. 'No, damn it. I never told you the truth.' He caught her arm and held her, his dark eyes blazing down into hers. 'But can you blame me? Before your accident you had cut me out of your life and, God help me, I wanted you. I love you. You must know I do!' He swore in exasperation.

Josie laughed in his face. Yesterday she would have exulted in his declaration of love, but today she knew better.

'No. The only thing you ever loved was the Beeches estate.' She stood only inches away from him, her body quivering with righteous indignation. 'Please don't insult my intelligence any further.' She watched a myriad of emotions flicker and fade in his eyes: anger, passion, humiliation. No, nothing could humiliate Conan; he was far too arrogantly male, *overwhelmingly* male. She must have imagined it, she thought dryly as his lips twisted in a cynical smile.

'You never believed me before your amnesia; why should I expect you to believe me now? But it was worth a try,' he drawled, and, letting go of her arm, he added, 'Go to bed; you look shattered. I'll sleep in the guest room, and we can discuss our future arrangements in the morning.'

Josie should have felt elated; she had won the argument. Conan was gone, and she was left with the anguish of her thoughts. She cringed with humiliation when she thought of the way she had abandoned herself to his lovemaking, and all the time he had been using her while waiting for Angela to return. Never again, she vowed silently. She would never forgive his betrayal.

CHAPTER TEN

SHE opened her eyes. Conan was standing by the bed, wearing only a navy blue towelling robe and holding a tray with a pot of tea and some toast on it. A smile parted her lips. 'For me?' Then she remembered.

'Get out of my room!' she snapped, sitting up in bed and eyeing Conan with disgust.

'No.' His gaze narrowed angrily on her mutinous face. 'You and I need to talk.'

'I have nothing to say to you, and I intend to leave here as soon as possible.'

'No, you're not. In the eyes of the world, we are a married couple expecting a baby, and that's the way it's going to stay.'

'Says who?' she taunted. 'The lying swine who pretended to be the father of my child, my lover?' It incensed her anew to think how he had tricked her.

'There was no pretence in our lovemaking; you enjoyed it as much as I did, and I never lied to you. I might have been economical with the truth, but I never lied.'

'You're unbelievable,' she fumed. 'I asked you straight out, if you were the only man I'd known, and you said yes.'

'Cast your mind back, Josie. I said you were a virgin when we *first* met, and you were. As I discovered the *second* time we met, when I found you in my bed,' Conan drawled sardonically.

Josie went red, then white at his reminder. 'Sophistry is obviously your strong point.'

'Maybe, but I'm not about to discuss my character with

you.' He was furious and it showed in his eyes as they raked over her pale features. 'All you need to remember is you are my wife, and you will behave as such. Hopefully, when you get over your childish resentment at what you see as my deceiving you, you will realise it's the best for everyone concerned. Until then we'll carry on as before.'

'No way!' Josie exclaimed. 'You are not sharing my bed, ever again. I'll sleep in the street before I'll let you touch me.'

'And this from the woman who declared I was her soul mate.' His mouth curled cynically. 'Don't worry, Josie, you have nothing to fear from me; my only intention is to fulfil my side of the bargain and look after you and the baby. And if you use your head for a moment instead of your hormones you'll realise you have to stay here with me. You have nowhere else to go,' he ended scathingly, and walked out.

He was right in one respect. She did not have anywhere else to live. Josie faced up to the truth, and the last of her illusions vanished. She was heavily pregnant, her father, who might have helped her, was halfway around the world, and Conan was powerful and determined enough to make her stay, whether she wanted to or not...

The weeks dragged past. Josie avoided Conan as much as she could, but he insisted on accompanying her to the doctor, and sat there displaying all the concerns of an expectant father, much to Josie's chagrin. They were coolly polite over dinner every evening, the only meal they shared. Josie spent most of her time reading in her bedroom. Pamela and Belinda called and they went shopping a couple of times, but basically Josie was trapped in Conan's home.

When she looked at Conan, tall and handsome, and aloof, she tormented herself with thoughts of him in bed with Angela, and then lashed out at him with scathing insults on his character, or lack of it. Her anger only intensified when he took all her snide remarks without comment.

Easter came and went, and with the arrival of the warmer weather Josie's frustration grew, as did her stomach. She felt like a duck waddling around.

Over dinner one night her frustration boiled over. 'I want to go to Beeches,' she declared. 'The renovations must be finished by now.'

Conan looked across at her, his expression inscrutable. 'Why?'

'To get away from you,' she shot back, but it wasn't true. Studying him through her lowered lashes, she realised Conan looked as tired and depressed as she felt, and she had an overwhelming urge to reach out to him and smooth the worry-lines from his broad brow.

That was really why she had to get away from him. If she didn't she was in danger of falling at his feet and begging him to love her.

Conan stood up and walked around to where she sat, and knelt by her chair, his head on a level with her own. She was so astonished that when he reached out and caught her hands in his she let him.

'Josie, I know you hate me, and you think you have good reason, but everything I have done, I have done for you and the baby.'

'Including sleeping with me?' she said coldly.

'And that's what bothers you most, isn't it? You can't forgive me for making love to you, but, worse, you can't forgive yourself for enjoying it.'

She tried to push back her chair and stand up. She did not need to hear this. But Conan's hands tightened on hers, his expression darkening angrily.

'You're not a child, although you've been behaving like one for the past few weeks, and I've let you get away with it because of your condition. I do understand how you feel, and I want to help. Tomorrow you have an appointment with Dr Masters. If the doctor agrees I'll take you down to Beeches this weekend when your father and the Major are due back. But only for a few days. Then you return here with me.'

'Your prisoner,' she snorted.

'No, your protector. I'm not an ogre, Josie, I'm your husband, and you're expecting your first baby in a few weeks. You're excited and afraid, and you need someone. That someone has to be me.'

'But...' Josie said huskily, touched against her will by the concern in his tone.

He captured her open mouth, stopping her objection, and started to kiss her tenderly, his tongue exploring her mouth with erotic delight, before he finally sat back on his haunches, his eyes smiling into hers.

'No buts... Nothing is as bad as it seems,' he said quietly, and stood up. 'Now go to bed before I forget my good intentions and carry you there.'

Josie's Thursday appointment with Dr Masters went without a hitch. Her blood pressure was a bit high, the doctor informed Conan, but was nothing to worry about, and while Josie struggled back into her clothes the doctor and Conan decided she could go to the Cotswolds for the weekend.

'Nice of the pair of you to consult me,' she sniped sarcastically at Conan on the drive home.

'Stop complaining, Josie; I'm not in the mood.'

She cast him a speculative look. His dark brows were drawn together in a deep frown, and he looked about as solitary and approachable as a tiger.

'Sorry if I've spoilt your day but you didn't have to come with me.'

'Yes, I did,' Conan said curtly as he stopped the car, and slid out. Walking around to the passenger door, he opened it, took her arm and helped her out. 'You may not want my help but you need it,' he declared, glancing at her protruding belly as he ushered her into the house. 'So no more arguing. I'm taking tomorrow off and we'll leave in the morning. Tonight I have a dinner engagement, which should cheer you up. You won't have to suffer my company any more today,' he snarled, and marched into his study, slamming the door behind him.

But for once Conan was wrong. Seven hours later Josie lay propped up in the delivery room of St Martin's clinic with Conan by her side, exhorting her to give one more push, and her baby was born.

Dr Masters placed the child in Josie's arms. 'Three weeks early but perfect. This little girl was certainly in a hurry to see the world.'

Josie lay back against the pillows and cuddled the infant to her breast, staring in awe and wonderment at the tiny face with a shock of black hair. Her daughter... She glanced up at Conan, standing by the bed, his gaze fixed on the infant in her arms. He looked out of place in the hospital, dressed in a black dinner suit.

'Thank you, Conan,' she said with heartfelt gratitude for his support, then, inexplicably shy, she added formally, 'I'm sorry Jeffrey called you away from your dinner.'

It had all happened so quickly; one minute she'd been in the bathroom getting ready for bed, the next her waters had broken, and she'd been panic-stricken. She had called for Jeffrey, and he had ordered the ambulance, and called Conan on his mobile phone.

'She's beautiful; I wouldn't have missed it for the world,' Conan murmured. 'A miracle... An absolute miracle.' He had been saying much the same thing all the time he had held Josie's hand in the delivery room, and insisted she remember her breathing exercises. 'She looks exactly like you, Josie. May I?' He leant forward and touched a gentle finger to the baby's cheek. 'Perfect.'

'She is, isn't she?' Josie agreed, yawning wildly, and with her eyes closing Dr Masters took the sleeping baby from her mother and handed her to Conan. Josie never saw the tears in her husband's eyes as she fell into a sleep of utter exhaustion.

When Conan walked into the room on Friday evening Josie was feeding the baby at her breast. She looked up as he entered. He was dressed casually in jeans and sweatshirt, and he stopped inside the door, his dark eyes fastened on the baby suckling on Josie's breast in stunned fascination.

'Conan.' Josie said his name softly.

His head shot up. 'Sorry for staring,' he said, a dull flush staining his hard-cut features.

'It's all right.'

Hesitantly he walked to the bed, and sat down on the chair provided for visitors. 'What are you going to call her?' he asked softly, glancing from the tiny baby to Josie's face and back again.

'I thought Kathleen, after my mother; it's from the Celtic and means dear to my heart.'

'Kathleen. Yes, I like it.' He looked up and caught the expression of pure love for her child in Josie's eyes, and his own darkened in some unidentifiable pain.

Josie, completely wrapped up in her baby, didn't notice.

It was the next day, when her father and the Major arrived, that her euphoric world took a knock.

'A girl!' the Major snorted. 'She looks nothing like a Zarcourt, though I suppose if Charles was alive he wouldn't have minded. She is a pretty little thing.'

Josie's eyes flew to where Conan was standing in the background. She saw him stiffen. His eyes were narrowed angrily on his father, and it suddenly hit her. Her troubles were not over with the birth of her child, but just beginning.

Her father, bless him, was much more enthusiastic. 'She's the image of your mother, Josephine, and I'm delighted you're going to call her Kathleen.'

But for Josie some of the joy went out of her heart at the Major's comment, and after the two older men left to travel on to Beeches she was too embarrassed to look at Conan.

'Take no notice of my father,' he said quietly, walking to the bed. 'Subtlety was never his strong point.'

'But he had the right to say it.'

'No, he did not. It's your baby and yours alone. No one has any right to the child but you.' His words should have cheered her up, but the reverse was true. Obviously Conan wasn't interested in the baby either.

Six weeks later Josie slid into the passenger seat of the sleek BMW and glanced at Conan sitting behind the steering wheel. Jeffrey was baby-sitting while Conan insisted on taking Josie to Dr Masters for her final check-up.

'There's really no need for you to accompany me,' she said for the hundredth time.

'I'm going with you and that's final.'

Silently fuming, Josie sat back and let her mind stray back over the past few weeks, and inevitably to Conan. Domineering and dangerous to her health, he was never far from her thoughts, however much she wished it were otherwise.

Her baby was a constant source of pleasure, but Conan was the opposite. Since the day she'd returned from the hospital, the gap between them had widened to a chasm. Josie could not look at him without remembering the intimacy they had shared, and the most intimate act of all— he had been present at the birth of her child.

In fact Josie saw very little of him. He was either at work or locked in his study, and he slept in the dressing room…

But several times when the baby had awakened in the night crying, to Josie's surprise Conan had appeared at the side of the crib, before she could even get out of bed. He'd cradled the child in his arms as if he really cared. Only last night Josie had finally put Kathleen to bed, and run herself a hot bath. Soaking in the tub, she'd thought she heard the baby cry and then there was silence. Five minutes later, dried and dressed in a towelling robe, she'd padded into the bedroom to find Conan, wearing only a pair of boxer shorts, leaning over Kathleen on the baby-changer, changing her nappy.

'You should have called me,' Josie had dashed to his side. 'You don't have to do that.'

'Maybe I want to,' he'd said quietly, and with a gentleness that was surprising in such a large man, he'd deftly dressed Kathleen, and, carrying her to her crib, laid her tenderly down to sleep. Straightening up, he'd turned back towards Josie, his dark eyes raking over her from top to toe, and back to linger where the vee of her robe revealed the soft swell of her breasts. 'And you needed to relax, I think.'

She'd looked up at him and heat had flooded through her whole body at the sensual knowledge she saw in the blackening depths of his eyes. Her figure had snapped back to normal with remarkable ease. If anything she was thinner than before except for her chest, but having Conan studying her so intently had sent her pulse rate sky-high.

'But nobody wants to change a nappy, certainly not a man like you,' she'd spluttered, dropping her gaze only to find herself staring at his half-naked body.

His mouth had tightened. 'What would you know about my wants?' he'd demanded scathingly. 'You believe I traded you for a lump of land; you don't know me at all.' And he'd walked out.

'We've arrived.' A harsh voice broke into her musing. Josie blinked and saw the car was parked outside the clinic.

Half an hour later Josie slid back into the car, her face scarlet with rage and resentment. Dr Masters had given her the all-clear, and had added that it was perfectly fine to resume normal sexual relations. Then Conan, his golden eyes glinting with devilment, had discussed the merits of different kinds of birth control with the doctor.

'What the hell did you think you were playing at?' she demanded, as soon as he got in behind the wheel, her eyes shooting flames. 'I have never been so humiliated—discussing birth control with Dr Masters, as if I didn't exist! You did it deliberately simply to embarrass me. We do not have a sexual relationship, nor will we ever again, as you know damn fine.'

He was silent for a long moment, his dark gaze penetrating. 'If you believe that, then you really are blind. I saw the way you looked at me last night. I know the sensual being that lurks beneath your Madonna-like exterior. Living together, it's only a matter of time before we end up in bed together.'

'Why, you arrogant swine!' She struck out with her hand but she was hampered by the close confines of the car and he easily captured her wrist, and held it pressed to his thigh.

'No, Josie, simply realistic. Dr Masters was very informative, and I thought you needed to know. After all, your past track record is not very good in that department,' he drawled with biting cynicism.

Josie couldn't believe he could be so cruel, reminding her of her one mistake—and anyway it wasn't a mistake; she loved her baby to bits. She stared at him with hatred in her eyes, and all her pent-up resentment came flooding out.

'But your track record with Angela, of course, is just great! Conan, her ever-present lover along with three husbands. Why don't you ask her to live with you again? She did before, and you won't have a problem. She told me herself she wouldn't get pregnant and spoil her figure, not even for you,' she sneered.

'You think I lived with Angela, I'm having an affair with her?' Conan exclaimed, his eyes widening in amazement on her furious face.

'I don't think. I know. Your precious Angela told me the very first time I met her that she'd lived with you, and if that wasn't enough she kindly passed on your message last year: how sorry you were. You were stuck in New York. And she was calling from London, and all the time telling you to be quiet in the background. The convenient wife in the country, and the mistress in the town. I'm nowhere near as blind as you would like me to be, buster.'

Conan stared at her for a long moment. 'You believe Angela and I...? That explains a lot.' Then he flung back his head and burst out laughing.

'Laugh as much as you like, but...'

'Ah, Josie,' he chuckled. 'You don't know how relieved I am. You're jealous!' he declared, his gold-flecked eyes capturing hers, and he curled her fingers into his palm. 'You have no idea how good that makes me feel.'

'Why, you big ape!' she yelled, pulling her hand from his. 'I am not jealous.'

'Josie, I have never lived with Angela. She borrowed my house with her brother while I was in New York. I have never been intimate with her. I respect her brain but I would sooner make love to a barracuda. And whatever she led you to believe over the telephone were lies.'

'So you say, but why should I believe you? At least Charles pretended to love me before taking me to bed. You just pretended I'd always slept with you, when I was in no fit state to know differently. You're not half the man Charles was.' She said it deliberately to hurt him, but she shrank back against the seat in real fear at the inimitable anger in his dark eyes.

The parking attendant knocking on the car window and gesturing them to move on stopped Conan's full response. 'Damn you!' he swore, and, turning the key in the ignition he crashed the gears and the car took off like a rocket.

Josie immediately wished the words unsaid. She wanted to apologise, but never got the chance. On returning to the house he instructed Jeffrey to pack what was needed, as they were leaving immediately for Beeches Manor, and three hours later he deposited Josie and the baby at the Manor House. He did not even stay for dinner but turned the car round and went back to London. His final terse words to Josie had been, 'You and Kathleen stay here. If you need anything, you have my telephone number; if I'm not there try the bank or Angela.' And with eyes as cold as the Arctic he'd left.

The hall looked light and airy in the morning sunshine. The whole house had taken on a new ambience since the renovations had been completed. When Josie had arrived three weeks ago, she had suffered shock upon shock. First her father and the Major had moved to the newly converted stable block at the back of the Manor. Mrs M. had her own apartment in the same block. The suite Josie had used the last time now had a nursery adjoining it. The estate manager, Mr Dorking, his wife and their three children had moved into Josie's old home, Low Beeches farmhouse.

Reaching the hall, Josie picked the mail up off the table on the way to the kitchen. She made herself a cup of coffee and sat down at the table to drink it. The first letter was junk mail, but the second left her sitting open-mouthed in shock. The official-looking document fell unnoticed from her hand. She couldn't believe it. From a firm of solicitors in Cheltenham, it was the deeds to the Beeches Manor estate made out in her name. Conan had given her the lot. But why? Mrs M. walked in and Josie glanced up at her, her face white as a sheet.

'How is Kathleen today?' Mrs M. asked.

'Fine, asleep,' Josie murmured distractedly.

'Are you all right? You don't look so good, lass.'

Josie looked at the older woman. 'A touch of baby blues,' she said—the first thing that came into her head. 'Since I've had to stop breast-feeding.'

'More like husband blues,' Mrs M. remarked caustically. 'When are you going to come to your senses and ring Conan? The poor man left here looking like his world had ended.'

'You don't understand,' Josie murmured, but she didn't understand herself. She looked down at the letter on the table, shaking her head in disbelief. Conan loved Beeches Manor. Why would he give it away?

'I understand better than you think. I know you've had a hard time the last few months, what with the accident and all. But these things happen and you have to get over them. Just look at this house. Conan has done everything for you, and you sit there indulging in self-pity over some stupid argument. It's time you snapped out of it and called him. You're a fool, Josie, if you let the past spoil the present. Conan is a proud man, and whatever you've argued about has hurt him deeply. It's up to you to put it right.'

'I don't want to discuss this,' she snapped, and groaned as Mrs M. walked out in a huff. Mrs M. did not know the half of it.

Josie picked up the letter and wandered out into the hall. She had heard nothing from Conan directly, but two days ago she'd received a bank statement, in her name, that had knocked her for six. She had felt like a kept woman, until she'd thought of her baby. Much as she hated accepting Conan's money, she was a mother first and her independence would have to wait until she was in a position to support herself without her child suffering. But this! She tapped the letter against her hand. This she could not accept. She glanced down at the telephone on the hall table, chewing nervously on her bottom lip.

Making up her mind, she picked up the receiver and dialled. She sighed with relief as Jeffrey's familiar voice answered. There was no point in rushing to London if Conan was not there. Five minutes later she replaced the receiver and went looking for Mrs Dorking.

By mid-afternoon Josie was bathed and dressed in a lilac silk sheath dress and toning high-heeled sandals. She planted a soft kiss on her baby's cheek before handing her to Mrs Dorking, who, with three children of her own, had no qualms about keeping Kathleen for the night. Josie stepped into her now repaired yellow car and started the engine.

On the drive to London, she had plenty of time to think about the past, and it slowly dawned on her that maybe she had been wrong about Conan. He had only ever shown her kindness and consideration from the day they married. He had been instrumental in helping her recover from the trauma of her ill-fated engagement to Charles. True, he had taken advantage of her when she'd had amnesia— But had he? She had wanted him just as much. Her jealousy over Angela he had dismissed with laughter, easily explaining the other woman's presence in his house. But she had not believed him, and had lashed out at him in the worst way. He had even said he loved her, and she had not believed that either. Dear heaven! If it was true, and she had denied him...

Jeffrey opened the door before Josie had a chance to knock, and within minutes he had her seated in the drawing room, and left to make some tea. Josie glanced around her.

Nothing had changed. She jumped to her feet and prowled around the room, too nervous to sit.

The door opened and, expecting Jeffrey, Josie froze as Conan strode in. His hand was at his throat, pulling at his tie, as he headed straight for the drinks cabinet, but something must have alerted him to her presence as he stopped in the middle of the room and turned to where she stood, frozen to the spot.

'You.' His dark eyes widened in surprise, quickly followed by fear. 'Has something happened to Kathleen?' he demanded, stepping towards her.

'No, No, she's fine. Getting bigger every day. She can smile now. Mrs M. insists it's just wind, but I know she smiles.' She was babbling, she knew, but the flood of emotions she felt at seeing Conan again had knocked every sensible thought from her head.

His dark hair was slightly longer, and his face a little thinner, but he was still the most attractive man she had ever met. As she watched he slipped off his jacket and flung it on a chair, and, carrying on to the drinks cabinet, he poured himself a large whisky.

'Do you want a drink?' he asked, his back to her.

'No, thank you.'

'Then what do you want?' he demanded coldly, turning around. One hip propped against the cabinet, he downed the drink in one go.

Her purse was on the sofa with the letter in it, she stepped forward to get it, and hesitated. Conan was watching her, his dark eyes roaming down over her slender body, and back to linger on the firm thrust of her breasts against the fabric of her dress, then slowly back to her face. What did she really want? she asked herself. Her violet eyes were doing some wandering of their own. He looked slightly rumpled and infinitely dear to her, and with a courage she had not known she possessed she walked across to him.

'I want you,' she said huskily, and, reaching out, she touched his arm.

'Want me?' He laughed harshly. 'Oh, please, Josie you must be desperate. What was it you called me? Half a man?' he drawled with biting sarcasm.

She lifted her eyes to his and was stunned by the angry bitterness she saw in their black depths. She had set out to hurt him that day, but only now did she realise how well she had succeeded. 'I'm sorry; I didn't mean it.'

'Yes, you did, Josie.' He slammed his glass down on the cabinet. 'The first time I tried to make love to you, you were thinking of him. I should have learnt then. But no, when the doctor told me you had lost your memory I quite ruthlessly took advantage of the fact to have you in my bed. Have you any idea what that did to me as a man? It almost destroyed me. Thinking every night, this is the last time; tomorrow she will remember. In the end it was relief when you did, knowing how low I had sunk in my desire for you.'

Looking back, Josie understood why she had thought he was withdrawing from her the last two weeks before her memory had returned. But the one thing that loomed large in her mind was that he had said he desired her. Standing close to him, her hand resting on his arm, she could feel the heat of his flesh through the fine silk of his shirt. 'Then so had I. Because I wanted you. Desired you. And still do,' she said quietly.

But she got no further as Conan grabbed her around the waist and hauled her tight against his hard body. His dark head swooped down and his mouth ground against hers in a savagely hungry kiss. He made no pretence of tenderness. His hands slid from her waist, curving one around her bottom, the other fondling her breast, while he spun her against the wall, nudged her legs apart and forced his thigh between hers.

'Please, Conan.' She pushed against him, but her body betrayed her as she trembled in his arms.

'Changed your mind again, sweetheart?' he snarled. 'Still hankering after Charles?'

'No, no. You don't understand. I never wanted Charles, not the way I want you. I never loved him,' she cried—and stopped. She had told him more than she'd ever wanted him to know.

Conan's grip tightened for a second. She felt the fierce tension tautening his huge frame and then abruptly he let her go, and if the wall had not been behind her she would have crumpled to the floor. 'Don't lie to me, Josie.' He took a step back but still he towered over her. 'I saw you, remember?' he prompted with biting cynicism. 'Or have you forgotten?'

She tilted her head back to stare into his dark eyes, as hard and unforgiving as sin. Something inside her snapped, and she lost it completely.

'Oh, I remember very well...too well,' she snarled. He was so bloody superior and she had had enough of feeling guilty. 'You want the truth? I'll give you the truth. I was a young girl with a crush on a blond-haired Adonis I had barely spoken to. The day Charles was supposed to be helping me at the church fête was the first time he asked me out. You were right. I went out with him three times in all, hardly a great love affair. Is that blunt enough for you?'

Conan went rigid, his eyes darkening with suppressed anger. That had got to him, she thought savagely, but she wasn't finished yet. 'The night I went to bed with him I'd had too much to drink, and I thought I loved him. When you found me lying on the bed, I wasn't glowing in the aftermath of love. I was thinking, If that's sex, it's horrible.' She didn't notice the narrowing of Conan's eyes, or the flash of some indefinable emotion contort his rugged face.

'The very next day, I think I knew I'd made a mistake,

because I wasn't even sad that Charles had left. If anything I was relieved. Three weeks later, after a few telephone calls from Charles, I was certain. Talking to him without his image to blind me, I knew we had nothing in common. Then I discovered I was pregnant. I love my baby and wouldn't be without her for the world. But the horrible truth is I never missed Charles at all, and I never intended to marry him.'

'And you expect me to believe you?' Conan said curtly.

His casual dismissal of her blunt confession was the last straw for Josie. 'I don't really care.' With her small chin jutting out belligerently she continued. 'I'm sick of feeling guilty. In fact I don't feel guilty any more. The first night you and I made love, the only reason I froze for a second was because I remembered the other time and was afraid. I tried to explain, but you wouldn't let me. It wasn't my fault you chose to think it was because I loved Charles.'

Josie didn't see the look of absolute horror in Conan's eyes. She laughed, a harsh sound in the momentary silence. 'In fact I should thank you for deceiving me into your bed when I had amnesia. Not remembering I had been afraid, by the time I discovered you'd tricked me, you'd certainly cured me of any inhibitions. Ironic, isn't it?' Suddenly the futility of arguing with him hit her, and, brushing past him she picked her purse up from the sofa. Opening it, she withdrew the letter.

'I actually came here to give you this.' Sitting down on the sofa, she held the letter out towards him. 'I don't understand you at all. You married me to get the Manor and now you're giving it away.'

Conan crossed the space dividing them in two lithe strides and, dropping down beside her, he grasped her by the shoulders. 'I don't want the Manor if I can't have you, and Kathleen as well. I married you for one reason only.

Because I love you. I used the excuse of getting the estate back to persuade you.'

She stared at him in shocked disbelief. 'But you said your father was going to leave it to me if I didn't marry you.'

'He might have said something along those lines, but as I held all the mortgages he had taken on the property over the years it was an empty threat. The first time I saw you, my reason for visiting Beeches was to make a deal with my father. I agreed to pay all his debts and he agreed to my taking over the Manor. The next time I saw you, Charles knew I was coming down that night to finalise the deal. So, you see, nothing could have persuaded me into marriage,' he declared huskily, 'Unless I wanted to.'

'So you didn't marry me to get the house?' Her heart turned over in her breast. 'I don't understand.' But she was beginning to.

'Oh, I think you do,' he said softly. 'I fell in love with you at first sight. I was driving past the vicarage garden, saw you and had to stop. When I approached you I was struck by your beauty, your innocence. I was so bewitched, I hadn't the sense to ask your name.' A bleak expression darkened his rugged features. 'Then Charles arrived and claimed you. I couldn't speak, I was so gutted, so I walked away.'

'Oh, Conan.' If only she had known, Josie thought.

'I know; childish of me. And later I was incensed with rage and jealousy when I discovered Charles had...' There was naked agony in his voice. 'Anyway, when he died it was tragic. But I saw my chance and took it. I was prepared to have you any way I could get you.'

Josie believed him; it was there in the fierce determination in his dark glance. This proud, arrogant man loved her and she was humbled at the thought.

'Oh, Conan if only I'd known,' Josie whispered, placing

her hand on his arm; the fact that he had been prepared to accept her unconditionally filled her with remorse. 'I've been such a fool and I was so jealous of Angela.'

'There was never anything between us, I swear.'

'I believe you.' She gazed into his dark eyes, her own deepening to purple, allowing all her love for him to show in their shimmering depths. 'And I love you quite desperately.'

Conan bent his head and their mouths met and clung, draining from each other every last bit of pain and anger in a passionate, deeply loving kiss. His arms tightened around her, and he lowered her back against the sofa. Raining tiny kisses over her face, he declared huskily, 'I love you, and baby Kathleen, more than life, and nothing else matters. I will never let you go again.'

Josie wrapped her arms around him, glorying in the length of his hard body pressing her down into the soft cushions, and buried her face against his neck. 'You are my life,' she whispered softly. 'I think I—'

'I've told you before.' Onc strong hand swept a few stray curls from her brow, and his dark eyes glinted with love and desire as he recognised the sensual gleam in her own. 'You think too much...' And for a long time they did not think at all.

A week later the whole village of Beeches crowded the church as Kathleen Devine Zarcourt was christened, her proud parents looking on with love...

HARLEQUIN PRESENTS®

EXPECTING

She's sexy, she's successful... and she's pregnant!

Relax and enjoy these new stories about spirited women and gorgeous men, whose passion results in pregnancies... sometimes unexpectedly! All the new parents-to-be will discover that the business of making babies brings with it the most special love of all....

September 1999—**Having Leo's Child** #2050
by Emma Darcy

October 1999—**Having His Babies** #2057
by Lindsay Armstrong

November 1999—**The Boss's Baby** #2064
by Miranda Lee

December 1999—**The Yuletide Child** #2070
by Charlotte Lamb

Available wherever Harlequin books are sold.

HARLEQUIN®
Makes any time special ™

If you enjoyed what you just read,
then we've got an offer you can't resist!

Take 2 bestselling love stories FREE!

Plus get a FREE surprise gift!

Clip this page and mail it to Harlequin Reader Service®

IN U.S.A.	IN CANADA
3010 Walden Ave.	P.O. Box 609
P.O. Box 1867	Fort Erie, Ontario
Buffalo, N.Y. 14240-1867	L2A 5X3

YES! Please send me 2 free Harlequin Presents® novels and my free surprise gift. Then send me 6 brand-new novels every month, which I will receive months before they're available in stores. In the U.S.A., bill me at the bargain price of $3.12 plus 25¢ delivery per book and applicable sales tax, if any*. In Canada, bill me at the bargain price of $3.49 plus 25¢ delivery per book and applicable taxes**. That's the complete price and a savings of over 10% off the cover prices—what a great deal! I understand that accepting the 2 free books and gift places me under no obligation ever to buy any books. I can always return a shipment and cancel at any time. Even if I never buy another book from Harlequin, the 2 free books and gift are mine to keep forever. So why not take us up on our invitation. You'll be glad you did!

106 HEN CNER
306 HEN CNES

Name _____ (PLEASE PRINT)

Address _____ Apt.# _____

City _____ State/Prov. _____ Zip/Postal Code _____

* Terms and prices subject to change without notice. Sales tax applicable in N.Y.
** Canadian residents will be charged applicable provincial taxes and GST.
 All orders subject to approval. Offer limited to one per household.
 ® are registered trademarks of Harlequin Enterprises Limited.

PRES99   ©1998 Harlequin Enterprises Limited

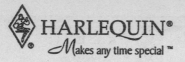

HARLEQUIN®
Makes any time special™

WIN A DREAM

In celebration of Harlequin®'s golden anniversary

Enter to win a *dream!* You could win:

- A luxurious trip for two to *The Renaissance Cottonwoods Resort* in Scottsdale, Arizona, or
- A bouquet of flowers once a week for a year from **FTD**, or
- A $500 shopping spree, or
- A fabulous bath & body gift basket, including K-tel's *Candlelight and Romance* 5-CD set.

Look for **WIN A DREAM** flash on specially marked Harlequin® titles by Penny Jordan, Dallas Schulze, Anne Stuart and Kristine Rolofson in October 1999*.

FTD

RENAISSANCE.
COTTONWOODS RESORT
SCOTTSDALE, ARIZONA

K-TEL

*No purchase necessary—for contest details send a self-addressed envelope to Harlequin **Makes Any Time Special** Contest, P.O. Box 9069, Buffalo, NY, 14269-9069 (include contest name on self-addressed envelope). Contest ends December 31, 1999. Open to U.S. and Canadian residents who are 18 or over. Void where prohibited.

PHMATS-GR